Allon
Book 10

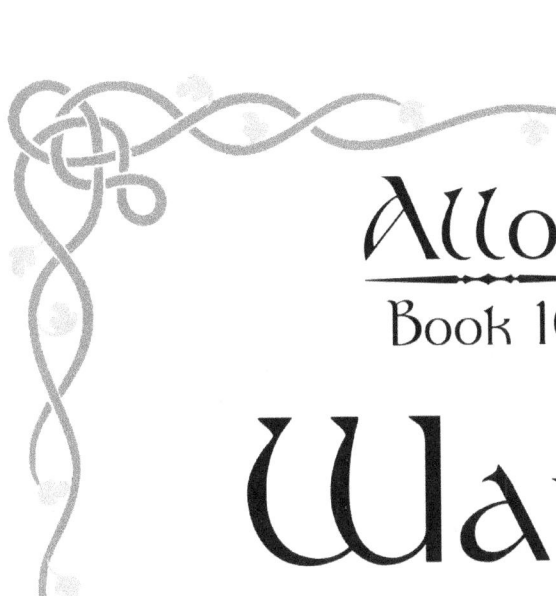

Waifs

10th Anniversary Novella

Shawn Lamb

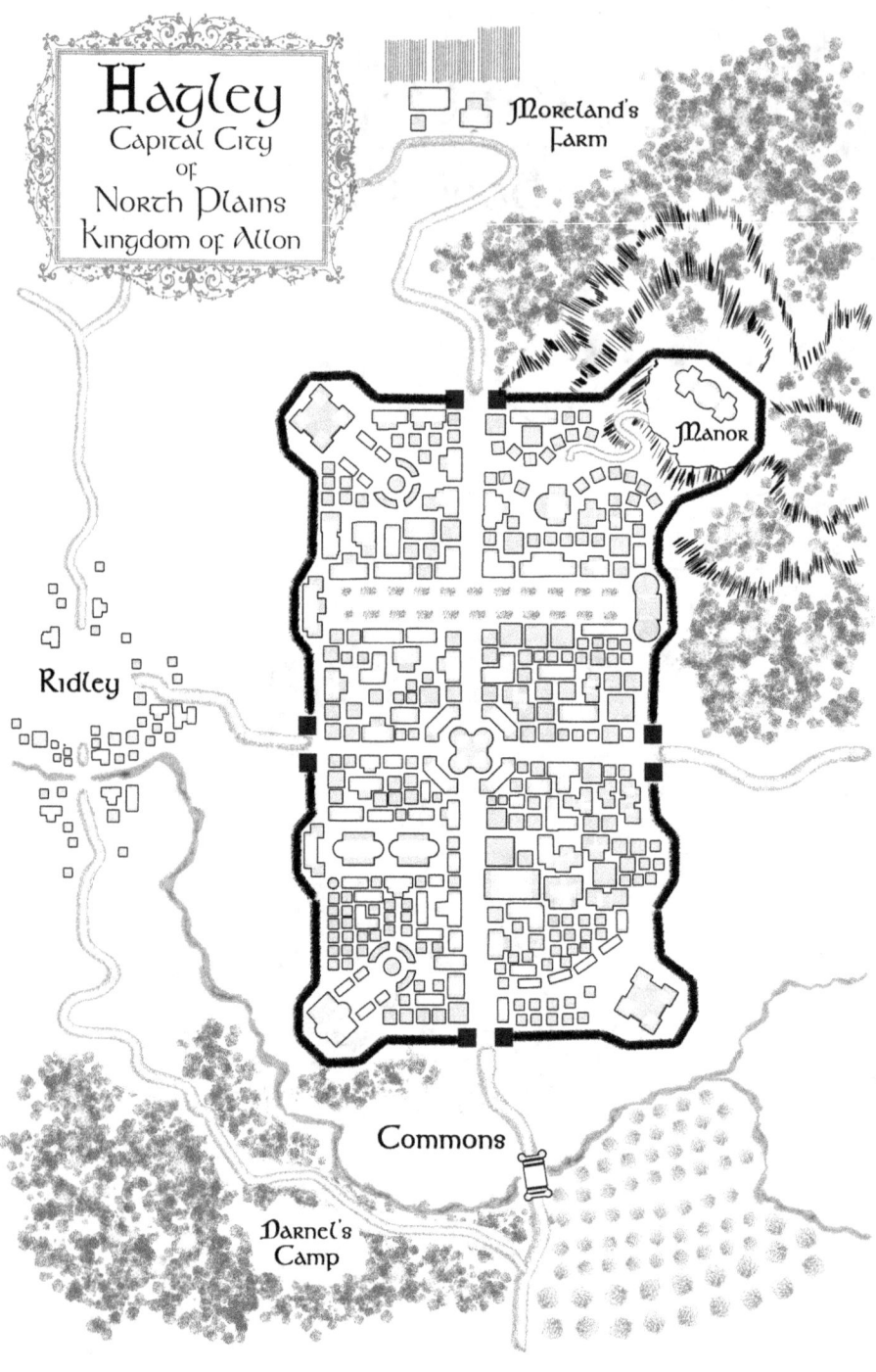

Hagley
Capital City
of
North Plains
Kingdom of Allon

Moreland's Farm

Manor

Ridley

Commons

Darnel's Camp

ALLON – BOOK 10 – WAIFS
10TH ANNIVERSARY NOVELLA
by Shawn Lamb

Published by Allon Books
209 Hickory Way Court
Antioch, Tennessee 37013
www.allonbooks.com

Cover illustration by Robert Lamb

Other Books by Shawn Lamb

Young Adult Fantasy Fiction

SON OF ELDAR
TRADER OF ELDAR – (SUMMER 2020)

ALLON – BOOK 1 – STRUGGLE FOR ALLON
ALLON – BOOK 2 – INSURRECTION
ALLON – BOOK 3 – HEIR APPARENT
ALLON – BOOK 4 – A QUESTION OF SOVEREIGNTY
ALLON – BOOK 5 – GAUNTLET
ALLON – BOOK 6 – DILEMMA
ALLON – BOOK 7 – DANGEROUS DECEPTION
ALLON – BOOK 8 – DIVIDED
ALLON – BOOK 9 – IN PLAIN SIGHT

GUARDIANS OF ALLON – BOOK ONE – THE GREAT BATTLE
GUARDIANS OF ALLON – BOOK TWO – REPRIEVE
GUARDIANS OF ALLON – BOOK THREE – OVERTHROW

PARENT STUDY GUIDE FOR ALLON ~ BOOKS 1-9
THE ACTIVITY BOOK OF ALLON

For Young Readers – ages 8-10
Allon – The King's Children series

NECIE AND THE APPLES
TRISTINE'S DORGIRITH ADVENTURE
NIGEL'S BROKEN PROMISE

Historical Fiction

GLENCOE
THE HUGUENOT SWORD

Royal Visitors

Prince Nigel, the King's Champion
Princess Mirit, wife of Prince Nigel, the Queen's Champion
Prince Eli, son of King Tyrone and Queen Tristine

Hagley

Sir Chad, Lord of the North Plains
Lady Magan, wife of Sir Chad
Master Platt, Director of the Hagley orphanage
Captain Dunsmore
Archie, butcher's apprentice, orphan
Burt, orphanage cook
Ike, a butcher

Outside Hagley

Alyson, orphan twin sister of Wyatt – age 11
Wyatt, orphan twin brother of Alyson – age 11
Darnel
Sophia, Darnel's wife
Vance, Darnel's eldest son
Genna, Vance's wife
Colby, Darnel's youngest son
Moreland, a farmer

Guardians

Avatar, Commander of the Elite Jor'ellian Guards
Virgil, a warrior
Skylar, a warrior, Overseer of Prince Eli
Mona, Trio Leader of the North Plains
Dale, a female ranger
Kendra, a scholar

Chapter 1

THE VIBRANT COLORS OF AUTUMN LEAVES STIRRED IN THE afternoon breeze. Prince Nigel, Princess Mirit, and young Prince Eli rode with Sir Chad to the walled city of Hagley. The city served as the capital of the North Plains, one of the twelve provinces of Allon.

Nigel and Mirit chose not to wear their uniforms as the King and Queen's Champions, rather rich royal traveling attire. After all, this was a holiday and not an official trip. Their nephew, fourteen-year-old, Eli, also wore casual clothes.

At age forty, Nigel kept himself in peak physical condition. His station as the King's Champion and First Jor'ellian Knight of the Temple demanded dedication and diligence. His golden-brown hair was trimmed and face clean-shaven. Keen blue eyes took notice of the surroundings. Years of conditioning taught him to make quick, decisive observations.

With Eli being the youngest son of Nigel's sister Tristine, family traits were visible in facial structure. Eli's hair was a few shades darker, while his eyes deep brown.

Although Mirit wore breeches, feminine touches accented her attire. Long auburn hair hung loose beneath the matching hat.

At age twenty-seven, Chad stood in marked contrast with bright red hair and vivid green eyes. After becoming Nigel's squire at age eight, he rose in the ranks of service. Last year, King Tyrone named him Lord of the North Plains.

The Guardian warriors, Virgil and Skylar accompanied the mortals. Virgil's light blond hair shimmered in the sunlight. Icy blue eyes shone with unnatural brightness, a trait common to Guardians. Skylar's neatly groomed golden locks reached his shoulders. His robin's egg-blue eyes remained watchful for the welfare of his charge, Eli. Both warriors had flawless skin and handsome features.

Guardians not only had unusual colored eyes, but also were endowed with perception equal to their heavenly station. At seven and a half feet, Virgil and Skylar towered above the mortals. They wore impressive swords and daggers, as they walked just behind Nigel, Mirit, Eli and Chad. Being accustomed to seeing Guardians, the populace took little notice of them.

The city streets thrived with commerce. Near a butcher shop, chickens squawked from small cages. Pig squeals came from a tightly packed pen. Merchants shouted about their wares to get attention from the passing throngs. The group turned north from the market to navigate the winding street toward Chad's home at the city's apex.

Passing a large self-contained establishment with an open archway, they heard the laughter of children. Younger ones played while older ones did chores.

"Are there more children than before?" Nigel asked.

"Sadly, there are," Chad answered, doleful.

A slender, clean-shaven man in his mid-fifties emerged from the archway. He hailed the group. "Sir Chad!"

Chad drew rein and turned in the saddle. "Master Platt."

In his urgency, Platt ignored Nigel, Mirit and Eli. "I was at the manor yesterday, only told you wouldn't be home until this evening, but you must know!"

"Know what?"

"Darnel is the in area," he spoke with dread anxiety.

Chad's brows leveled with chagrin. "You've seen him?"

"No, Archie did while fetching wood for lumber. He hurried back to tell me."

"Who is Darnel?" asked Nigel.

"A hard-bitten brute of a man, who only sees orphans as profit," chided Platt, though his focus remained on Chad. "I spoke to Lady Magan and Captain Dunsmore."

7

"Good. Dunsmore will see there is an extra patrol of the orphanage area. Now, what about the special provision I left?"

"Oh," began Platt caught off guard at the change of subject. He then smiled. "The children were so excited, yet disappointed by your absence."

"I'll stop by tomorrow, and with their Highnesses."

Platt colored with embarrassment at finally taking notice of Nigel. "Oh, Highness, I didn't recognize you. I'm sorry."

Nigel chuckled. "I understand your concern is for the children."

"He does look different out of uniform," teased Mirit.

"You're very generous, Princess," said Platt with a slight bow. "I know the children look forward to seeing both of you." He slyly grinned at Nigel, "The boys still speak of the Champion's—"

Nigel raised a swift hand. "Ahh!" he said yet kept a bantering tone. "We have vowed to never speak of that again, Master Platt."

Mirit and Chad fought to contain their laughter, which piqued Eli's interest.

"Speak of what, Uncle?"

Nigel made the same curt teasing gesture to his nephew.

Platt fought to curb his amusement. "As you say, Champion."

"Until tomorrow, Master Platt." Chad kicked his horse to continue their trek.

"What was that about?" Eli quietly asked Mirit.

"I'll tell you later," she said with a mischievous grin.

Nigel ignored them to move his horse beside Chad. "This Darnel poses a threat to the orphanage? How?"

"Not the orphanage, the orphans. He's not exactly a slave trader but snatches unsuspecting orphans to sell or barter to farmers, merchants, or whomever will pay for them."

"How is that not a slave trader?" asked Mirit with offense.

"Slaves usually have families they were taken from, or those separated during a sale. Darnel targets those without families. The defenseless, whom no one will miss or attempt to find. This enables him to circumvent the law since no one will press charges."

"That's horrible!" chided Eli. "He should be arrested and charged."

"He will. Once I find him." Chad's jowls flexed with painful anger.

Nigel noticed the harsh expression along with the strident tone. "How did you end up at the farm you ran away from before we met?"

Chad briefly pursed his lips before replying. "Someone like Darnel. One day, while playing, I wandered too far from the orphanage. The next thing I knew, I was in a wagon that took me far from any place familiar. I don't know the bargain made, as he just left me with the farmer."

"How old were you then?" asked Mirit.

"Six. I became an orphan at age five. I was eight when I met Nigel."

"After a year of wandering the roads," added Nigel.

Mirit's visible disturbance increased, so Chad said, "It was a long time ago. My life has taken many unexpected turns since. Still, I haven't forgotten where I came from."

"Your generosity and patronage of the orphanage is a testament to that," said Nigel.

"I've simply built upon what Malcolm started."

"Done with the heart of one who knows."

"Ay." Chad again went to change the subject. "Today I am blessed with a good wife, and now a third son, who I can't wait for you to meet."

"We could hardly stay away after receiving the news that you named him *Niki* after our Tunlund escapade." Nigel winked at Chad.

"He did not," said Mirit in lighthearted refute.

"Better Niki than *Yitzak*," said a new voice from behind.

They turned to see another Guardian had joined Virgil and Skylar.

"Avatar," said Mirit with delight. "What brings you here?"

Avatar grinned. His bronze hair and goatee contrasted his shiny silver eyes. Instead of the warrior's daily tan uniform, he wore a white and gold uniform with purple trim for his station as Commander of the Jor'ellian Guard. "When I heard you and Nigel were coming to Hagley, I decided to join you."

"Avatar is a frequent visitor," Chad explained.

Virgil spoke to Avatar. "*Yitzak* means a joke. Why would anyone use that for a child's name?"

9

Nigel heartily laughed. "That was Avatar's name for our Tunlund mission."

Virgil and Skylar fought the impulse to laugh.

"Wasn't Tunlund where you rescued Titus?" asked Eli.

"Ay," replied Avatar. "The name wasn't my choice," he stressed to his Guardian comrades.

"Nor was being shaved and having your ear pierced," said Chad.

Virgil and Skylar lost the battle, and heartily laughed.

"According to the king," began Avatar flippantly to his fellow Guardians, "Nigel couldn't wait to get away from Waldron after enduring Titus' wedding."

"Really?" asked Chad, a bit surprised.

With an embarrassed frown, Nigel admitted, "Ay. I don't know which was worse—Titus' jitteriness or Tristine's fussing. I've never seen her so nit-picky. Even Tyrone had difficulty pleasing her demands." He quickly spoke to Eli, "Don't tell your mother."

Eli wryly smiled. "Why do you think she suggested I accompany you?"

"Tristine knows?" Nigel asked with surprise.

Mirit giggled. "You can't fool the women in your life."

"She's not with child again, is she?" asked Chad.

"No. Father believes it is because her eldest got married."

Nigel shrugged with indifference. "It's as good excuse as any for a woman to use."

"I hope she doesn't act so when I get married," Eli complained.

They arrived at the manor. It sat upon the highest point in Hagley overlooking the city and surrounding countryside. Grooms rushed to greet them and take the horses. The steward joined the grooms.

"Ambrose. Has the royal baggage arrived?" Chad asked,

"Ay, my lord. The apartment is ready, Highness." Ambrose bowed to Nigel and Mirit. "My lord," he paid respects to Eli.

In the foyer, they met Magan, Chad's wife. A tall, slender woman with pleasant features, raven hair and hazel eyes.

"Highness. I'm so glad you could come." She went to make the customary bow when Mirit embraced her.

"Don't stand on ceremony. You know we seek every opportunity to visit." She took Magan's arm to move further into the house. "How was your labor?"

"Easier than the twins." With a large smile, Magan looked over her shoulder to Chad. "He has his father's red hair, fine ginger lashes, only blue eyes."

"Did you name him Niki?" Mirit asked in a teasing tone.

"We thought about it," Magan joined in the fun.

The others laughed while Nigel huffed a wry chuckle.

"Truth be told, I chose Nigel," said Chad.

Surprise brought Nigel to a halt. "What?"

"Did you really name him Nigel?" asked Mirit.

"We compromised. Magan wanted to honor her father Leslie, so we combined them and named him Niles."

"My great-grandfather," said Nigel.

"Sir Niles of Pollux," Eli said in a statement rather than question seeking confirmation.

"Ay," Nigel replied with fond remembrance. "Mother spoke very highly of him. He helped Father on his quest to restore the House of Tristan. Alas, Dagar killed him before he could see my parents crowned."

Chad gripped Nigel's arm. "I know. We felt it fitting. If it isn't too presumptuous?" He spoke in a tone suggesting he knew the answer.

Nigel tossed an arm about Chad's shoulder. "This calls for a toast!"

Chad began to steer Nigel to the drawing room when Mirit's inquiry stopped them.

"Can we see him first?"

"Don't you want to rest from the trip?" asked Magan.

"No. I'd like to see him."

"Why not? It's not every day I have half-a-namesake. Lead on," said Nigel.

Magan took them upstairs to the nursery. Three-year-old twin boys, Chandler and Ephrim, happily played in a corner. Both were brown headed with brown eyes. Two nurses attended them while a third woman sat beside a cradle.

"Papa!" Chandler ran to Chad. Ephrim quickly followed.

Chad got down on one knee to greet his sons. "I told you I would only be gone a couple of days." He stood and held each boy by the shoulder. "What do you say to His Highness?"

"Good day, Highness," they said in unison while attempting bows.

"Good day, Masters Chandler and Ephrim," Nigel formally replied.

"Oh, silly men. Come here, boys." Mirit knelt. The twins giggled when they hugged her. "How you both have grown."

"I'm bigger! Ephrim puffed out his chest, which made Chandler scowl. Ephrim pointed to the cradle. "Baby brother." He took Mirit's hand to lead her across the room.

"Ephrim's talking more," Nigel commented to Chad.

"Ay. Eldric's treatment has helped, along with Avatar's suggestion of taking individual time with the boys." With a fond smile, Chad regarded the twins. "I've learned much about my sons during those separate times. It's also helped me understand their interactions when together. The dynamic is so different apart and together."

"Chandler's dominant personality was overwhelming Ephrim," Avatar explained to Nigel's curiosity.

"Ay," agreed Chad. "Ephrim is more relaxed and confident when alone." He motioned to Avatar with an affirming nod. "After a few months of our sessions, he has begun to counter Chandler when Chandler becomes too aggressive."

"Oh," they heard Mirit cooed. She lifted Niles out of the crib. "He's so adorable. Nigel, look." The baby made contented noises; wide blue eyes opened.

"A good-looking baby." Nigel gently touched the infant's cheek. With a tiny hand, Niles grabbed Nigel's finger. "Strong too."

Mirit glanced to Chad. "He does look like you."

"Me!" Ephrim tugged on Mirit's pant leg.

"Of course. He looks like his big brother also."

"That makes three." Chandler held up three fingers.

Niles started to grow fussy and screwed up his face.

"He just woke from his nap and needs to be changed." The nurse took him from Mirit.

"Come. Refreshment is waiting," said Magan.

Nearing the door to leave, they hear loud squeals from the twins. The boys decided to attack Avatar. They buzzed about his legs. The Guardian played along with their antics.

"Boys," Chad half-scolded, but they continued their playfulness. "They do this to him every time, and he indulges them."

"I did the same. Take down the Guardian," said Nigel.

As if on cue, Avatar pretended to fall to one knee. Chandler climbed on his back. Virgil went to join in, when Chandler snapped, "No!"

"Chandler!" Chad sternly rebuked.

The boy tried to get down, only ended up falling. He became upset, so Avatar set him on his feet.

"Virgil was just trying to play," said Avatar. When Chandler looked skeptically at Virgil, Avatar continued, "Don't pout. You know Virgil."

With a lively shout, Ephrim snatched Virgil around the leg in an attempt to tackle him. He wasn't having much success.

"Ouch!" exclaimed Virgil when Ephrim bit him in the leg. He swiftly detached the boy from him.

"Boys, that's enough!" Chad seized them each by an arm. He glared at one of the women. "Have they had their nap today? They are unusually rambunctious."

"No, my lord. With all the preparations for arrival … I'm sorry." She took a hand of the sulking twins to lead them to their beds on the other side of the chamber.

Once in the hallway, Chad spoke. "My apologies, Virgil. Are you hurt?"

"No, though I can't recall being bitten by a mortal before. He has strong teeth."

"I recall someone else doing the same to me at that age." Skylar sent a sideways glance to Eli. The teenage prince flashed a toothy grin.

Downstairs, they entered the private family dining room. "I prepared a special meal. One I know you shall enjoy," said Magan.

"We always enjoy your cooking," said Nigel.

Chad widely grinned. "This is extra special. I managed to get Joby's venison recipe. Or rather, Wess wormed it out of him by citing you wanted to find a way to have it prepared for the King."

Nigel smacked his lips. "Magan, if you have mastered the recipe, then the next time Tyrone comes to hunt stag in the province, he will be drooling."

Although food and drink were not necessary to Guardians, they partook of the celebratory toast and meal.

After the last course of supper, Nigel sat back with a satisfied sigh. "Magan, you equaled Joby in preparation."

"Indeed," agreed Avatar. "Even Armus will be jealous," he said of the Guardian Second-in-Command, known for his acquired culinary skills.

Magan beamed. "Thank you, Highness. Commander."

"Magan," began Nigel in kind reproof. "How many times must we tell you, there is no need to be formal in private? You are now Lady Magan, wife of a Jor'ellian Knight and member of the Council. You can call us by our names."

Magan awkwardly shrugged. "I'm still getting used to it. Being brought up around the Temple and Fortress, there weren't many informal occasions. We've been so busy establishing Chad as the new provincial lord we haven't really entertained guests. Other than you and Her High—Mirit, only the Count, Wess and Vivian have visited us."

Avatar made a light clearing of his throat. He poured cider more cider into his tankard.

"Avatar visits frequently," she added.

"He can hardly stay away from the boys," Chad quipped.

Avatar chuckle into the tankard as he drank.

"How many times have they bitten you?" Virgil asked.

"Never. I learned how to avoid it after dealing with Nigel. Teething is the worse time." Avatar held up his right hand. "He tried to use my fingers as chew toys."

Nigel heartily laughed, as did Magan, Eli and Chad, only Mirit seemed subdued to the humor. The reason became obvious when she asked, "Why has the number of children increased at the orphanage?"

The abrupt change in subject, momentarily caught Chad off-guard. "This year's summer and early fall rains may have helped to relieve the two-year drought, but by then it had taken its toll on the poor, and some smaller farms. Hagley's population has swelled from fifteen thousand to almost twenty-one thousand. Many moved to the city for relief. Malcolm tried his best, but in fragile health, and the unfortunate war, well, you see the consequences."

"Tyrone sent royal engineers and nature Guardians to help Malcolm," said Nigel.

"Ay. The aqueducts, canals and reservoirs are completed. Rainwater is now being stored for future irrigation. However, construction suffered interruption when diverting manpower and material for battle."

"Some who sought refuge lost their lives in the war leaving behind children," said Magan, somberly.

"Thus, the need for a second orphanage," added Chad. "Platt is at capacity with eighty. His brother and his wife took in those who are unadoptable."

"Unadoptable?" asked Eli with some confusion.

"The blind, deaf and some …"

"Crippled," Nigel finished when Chad hesitated.

"Ay," Chad slowly admitted then added, "Be assured, they are well cared for. Platt's brother, Grady, has infinite patience, along with a gentle soothing manner. They will be joining us tomorrow on the commons, so you can see for yourself."

Seeing Mirit's preoccupied forlorn expression, Nigel stretched with a partial yawn. "Well, it's been a long day. I think an early night is in order."

"Your chambers are prepared. Ambrose lit fires for the water reservoir, should you desire to bathe," said Magan.

Mirit's smile didn't reach her eyes. "The meal was delicious. Good night."

Upstairs, the couple's guest apartment consisted of two rooms connected by an archway and a separate door. The archway divided the dressing room from the sleeping area. The door led to a privy. With a soft-spoken word, Mirit dismissed the servants waiting to tend them. She made her way to the dressing area where nightclothes and evening toiletries were properly arranged. She took off her doublet and boots.

"Perhaps we shouldn't have come," said Nigel.

She didn't respond rather gathered the nightclothes to head toward the dressing screen.

He intercepted her. "I know it's difficult for you, but you must accept it will never happen."

"I have accepted it. I admit, I still grieve on occasion that I can't … that we can't have children."

"It's not *on occasion*. I see the longing in your eyes each time you hold an infant." When she shied away, he gently turned her back. "I do understand. I too have felt an emptiness from time to time." He caressed her cheek. "Yet, when I think about the choice of either you or children, there is no choice." He continued when she went to object. "I know you don't recall what happen, but I do! Even after all these years, there are times the haunting images of seeing you stuck down creep into my dreams."

"I know. Those nights you cling to me," she softly said.

He bent his head, so their foreheads touched. "I thank Jor'el he restored you to me. Children would be an added blessing, but," he began to smile, "after nearly chewing off Avatar's fingers and seeing Ephrim bite Virgil, I'm easily dissuaded by the violence of children."

She playfully struck him. "What about you? Chad tried to be discreet when mentioning the crippled orphans."

16

"I'm well past that part of my life. Although I am touched by those infirmed, it doesn't burden me anymore. I can willingly interact with them without personal remorse or self-pity. Can you tolerate going to orphanage?"

"And disappoint the children? No. I will make every effort to keep it from affecting my attitude."

"That's my girl." He kissed her.

Chapter 2

THE NEXT DAY AT BREAKFAST, MIRIT WAS IN BETTER SPIRITS.
"I received a note from Master Platt earlier this morning."
Chad's smiling glance passed between Mirit and Nigel. "The
children look forward to the Champion—"

Nigel made a negative grunt when he put up a hand. "Remember the
vow."

"You have to admit it was very amusing," Mirit teased.

"I don't have to admit anything of the kind."

Hearing Avatar laugh, Nigel sarcastically said, "So that's the reason
you're here, to see if I humiliate myself again."

"You mean, lend a helping hand." Virgil nudged Avatar, who didn't
bother to hide his amusement.

Feigning offense, Nigel chided Avatar. "You set me up!"

"No, I merely helped facilitate your initiation."

The answer baffled Nigel. "Initiation into what?"

"The secret society. They were testing you. You passed when you
accepted the *accidental* humiliation with humor."

Nigel wryly grinned. "I've been tested many times before, but this is
the first I can recall by children."

"Orphans," corrected Avatar, a bit more serious.

"He's right," said Chad. "Many are skeptical of adults."

"Why?" asked Eli.

Chad tried to be discreet. "Many have had bad experiences with
adults."

"You mean abuse?"

With a lamenting sigh, Chad nodded. "It is a sad, cruel fact of life, inflicted upon many orphans."

Under furrowed brows of distress, Eli stared at the table. "Such a reality is hard to imagine when I've been so blessed with a loving family. Though how could a parent, or any adult, abuse a child?"

Chad's brow grew shrouded. "That is a question many have asked, and with no satisfactory answer. The situations vary, but the result is the same: fear and skepticism."

"You weren't fearful of me," said Nigel. "In fact, I tried everything to chase you away because I knew the danger, only you were persistent."

Chad shrugged. "I don't know why, only that something drew me to you."

"Jor'el," said Avatar.

Chad nodded. "I realized that years later. Being eight at the time, all I saw was a cripple, a fellow outcast in need of aid. I never thought I would help thwart a coup." He turned to Nigel. "When Musetta struck you down, I started to rush in to help but became blinded by light. When I could see again, Avatar stood there protecting you and Tristine."

"All the same, I never felt you were testing me."

"No, but some orphans aren't so easily convinced, especially if their experiences are more traumatic then mine. They view adults as the enemy. I know the orphans in Platt's care accepted you, because they changed the picking day upon learning you and Mirit were coming to visit."

"Picking day? You mean the apples?" asked Mirit.

"Ay. They are a week overdue. Havelock left them some choice apples after the harvest."

Magan tried to allay the sensitive subject. "I have venison meat pies baking. Something to help should you be tested again."

Nigel laughed. He then turned to Avatar. "Any plans I should know about?"

"I'm just the facilitator not the planner."

"I don't suppose you'll give me warning?"

"And spoil their amusement?"

"Or your own entertainment," quipped Skylar.

Avatar simply drank.

Captain Dunsmore led a platoon of mounted soldiers to the commons outside the city. A large, strong man of fifty, and every inch a soldier, with a neatly trimmed, grey speckled, black hair and thin beard.

"Master Platt," he hailed.

"Captain. Is his lordship not with you?"

"He and the others shall be along shortly. I came to inspect the preparations." He gently smiled, as he watched the children at work and play.

"All is going well. Have you seen any sign of Darnel?

Dunsmore shook his head. "Not yet. I have men stationed on the perimeter should he try to disturb the festivities."

"Master Platt! Master Platt!" An older girl came running. Almost out of breath, she pointed behind her.

"What is it, Debra?"

She couldn't speak well for running. "There … Him!"

Dunsmore didn't need any further explanation. "First three with me!" He spurred his horse to gallop in the direction indicated. The soldiers obediently complied.

A half-mile from the picnic area, they came upon an encampment of two wagons. The occupants, three men and two women, seemed unconcerned at the sight of soldiers. The men ranged in age from twenty to fifty-five, while the women mirrored the men on the age spectrum. All wore modest clothes.

Dunsmore's horse skidded to an abrupt halt. He glared at the eldest male of the group. "Darnel. You were warned about returning to Hagley."

"I'm not in Hagley, Captain, rather on common land," Darnel replied in an accent that told of a Highland heritage. His voice matched his sturdy frame with dark grizzled hair and beard.

"All the same, you're not welcome here."

"The last I heard common land was free from noble harassment. Or has the King ordered otherwise?"

"The King has not. Beware, Darnel, the Champion is here. He won't tolerate your kind of behavior."

"What behavior is that, Captain? Partaking of a pleasant autumn day? Same I see happening yonder."

Dunsmore's glance shifted between the picnic and Darnel. "If you value the continuation of your freedom, stay clear of the festivities. My men are watching." Not waiting for a reply, he turned his horse to gallop back to the picnic.

Upon return, Dunsmore found Chad, Magan and the others spoke with Platt. For the day, Mirit and Magan wore breeches with feminine tailoring. Chandler and Ephrim were eager to join the other children. When the twins broke away from their mother, Eli acted.

"I'll watch them." He ran after the boys.

Chad took brief notice of Eli's departure, more concerned with Dunsmore's harsh expression. "Trouble, Captain?"

"Darnel. About a half-mile west. Men are stationed on the perimeter. I also made certain he is aware of the Champion's presence." He nodded toward Nigel.

"Why not make him leave?" asked Magan.

"Because, my lady, he is within his rights to be on common land. Inside Hagley, I can arrest him for trespassing due to his lordship's orders. Out here, the King's law rules."

"I understand the difference, Captain. I am not suggesting you violate the King's law, merely concern for the children's safety."

Dunsmore tolerantly smiled. "As am I, my lady. He and his companions so much as step a foot past the perimeter, I have the authority to act in protection of all here."

"Thank you, Captain."

"My lady." Dunsmore touched his hat in salute. He left.

"Dunsmore is a very accomplished officer. I know Malcolm relied heavily upon him," Nigel said to Magan.

She spoke in sheepish reply. "I know. He has been most kind and helpful while I adjust. As I said, my concern is for the children."

"Speaking of." Platt indicated where almost one hundred children gathered in sort of a formation with the smallest and youngest in front, the older ones in back. Many wore large smiles while a few seemed uncertain. "They are ready to receive the honored guests."

"We shouldn't keep them waiting." Mirit took Nigel's hand to approach the children.

Virgil, Skylar, and Avatar began to follow when Virgil abruptly stopped. He turned to the knoll. No one was there.

"Something wrong?" asked Avatar.

"I thought I sensed ... a presence."

Avatar's eyes narrowed in concentration. "I don't sense anyone."

Befuddled, Virgil shook his head. "It was quick and fleeting. Not discernable enough to identify."

"Maybe Darnel, since the mortals believe he poses a threat," suggested Skylar.

Virgil pursed his lips in consideration. "I'm usually not that attuned to mortal schemes."

"Just your charge," Skylar teased, only Virgil didn't respond to the humor.

"We'll keep our senses sharp," Avatar assured Virgil.

Upon hearing laughter of children, they saw Nigel and Mirit surrounded by the orphans with enthusiastic greetings.

"Don't tell them about this. It could be nothing. If something else happens, then we can speak," said Virgil.

In agreement to keep quiet, they joined the mortals.

A ginger-headed boy of thirteen teased Nigel. "You're not wearing your uniform, Champion."

"One dousing is enough to learn my lesson, Archie. Besides, this isn't a formal visit, rather a holiday."

"Then welcome, Your Highness." Archie made an amused bow then continued his light-hearted banter. "Will you participate in the games again?"

"What have you planned, my clever one?"

"Oh, just the usual test of skill and balance."

"He's improved since last year." Dunsmore gave a friendly clap on Archie's neck. The boy proudly smiled.

Nigel caught sight of Avatar's arrival. "By yourself or did you have help?"

Avatar tried to keep the smile from his face, as he carefully shook his head at Archie.

"By myself, Highness. Same as last year, right, Captain?"

Dunsmore laughed. "Don't drag me into your secret."

"I know your secret," chuckled Nigel.

Archie's smile grew. "Perhaps in execution, but not planning. However, this year I will defeat you cleanly since it will be my last."

"Last?"

"I'm to be adopted," Archie happily announced.

"By whom?" asked Mirit with great pleasure.

"By me, Princess," replied Dunsmore. "And you can call me Papa, not captain," he said to Archie.

"Rather unusual since the captain isn't married," interjected Platt, a bit hesitant. He changed his tone after an admonishing glare from Chad. "A fine choice, considering his upstanding character."

Dunsmore confronted Platt. "You know I've been trying to adopt Archie since he arrived three years ago." He explained to Nigel and Mirit. "Despite my bachelorhood, we have bonded. However, Lord Malcom wasn't well enough to accommodate me. Sir Chad has been most helpful. All we need is his signature on the papers."

"Chad nothing! I will sign it," said Nigel cheerfully. "And put this seal next to the King's seal." He indicated his Jor'ellian signet ring. "A double sign of royal and divine agreement."

Archie widely smiled. "Thank you, Highness!"

"My pleasure." Nigel leaned closer to speak with an impish smile. "Yet know this, clean or not, I will defeat you."

Archie flashed a glance to Avatar then replied to Nigel. "I'll let you win for old time's sake."

Avatar heartily laughed.

"Archie!" Another older boy waved to him.

He waved back. "Preparations," he told Nigel before leaving.

"I'm glad to hear about Archie, for I see many new faces," said Mirit. A girl of six tugged on her leg. She held large apple up to Mirit. With a tender smile, Mirit picked up the girl. "Corinna. You eat. I'll get another apple."

"I remember you." Nigel tickled her, which made her giggle and cuddle up to Mirit.

"I wonder why she's still here, as cute and loving as she is." Mirit kissed Corinna's forehead. The girl concentrated on trying to eat the apple.

Debra approached. "Excuse me, Highness, but it's time for Corinna's medicine." She reached to take the girl from Mirit.

"I didn't know she had been ill."

Debra expression turned fretful. She shook her head before she left with Corinna.

The action disturbed Mirit. "Master Platt. What is her illness?"

His somber expression told the answer before he spoke. "I'm afraid it is incurable, Princess. It's a miracle she has lived another year."

Mirit fearfully stared in the direction Debra left. "Are you certain it is fatal?"

"Sir Chad sent for Lander, whom Eldric assigned as the province's Guardian physician. He confirmed her condition and calls upon the orphanage once a month to examine her and the other children. She is unaware anything is wrong. She is well-cared-for and wants for nothing."

Despite Platt attempted to reassure her, Mirit fought to contain her distress. "I'm certain you are doing what is best."

At that moment, Mistress Platt and Burt, the orphanage's cook, summoned everyone to supper. As honored guest, Nigel offered a blessing for the feast.

"I thought the venison pies were to be his consolation prize in case of defeat," Virgil quipped to Avatar when Nigel put two of the smaller pies on his plate.

Nigel heard. "Fortification for strength to face what challenges await me."

Chapter 3

ACROSS THE CREEK NEAR THE BRIDGE, WYATT AND ALYSON HID in the bushes to watch the festivities. They were eleven-year-old twins with similarly smudged features, flaxen hair and hazel eyes. Their clothes were old and tattered in places. He licked his lips, as he stared at the food. He started to move out of their hiding place when she snatched him.

"We can't just go over there."

Wyatt made a shrugging gesture for *why?*

"That's why." She pointed to the soldiers that either stood watch or sat upon horses at various intervals along the creek. "We'll wait until it gets dark. Maybe there'll be some food left."

He deeply frowned and held his stomach.

"I know. I'm hungry too. We'll just have to wait. I promise, we'll get something to eat."

With the meal done, the games began. The smaller children played tag or hide-and-seek. This included Chandler and Ephrim. The older boys convinced Eli to join in feats of skill and daring. Nigel and Chad served as referees for the older boys. The girls participated in less demanding sports like bobbing for apples or running while balancing an apple their head. Mirit and Magan joined the girls. Virgil, Skylar, and Avatar delighted the very young with Guardian tricks and feats of strength.

All gathered for the final event; climbing an obstacle course constructed over the deepest part of the creek. Archie and Nigel were pitted against each other, the same as last year. Nigel removed his doublet while Archie took off his jacket.

At the starting line, Archie asked, "Ready, Highness?"

"Any pig grease this year?" Nigel bantered in return.

The youth grinned. "I told you I would win cleanly. Not that I cheated last year." He tossed a look back to where Avatar stood with a small boy of five on his shoulders.

The boy giggled at the height. "I can see everything!"

"This year you won't miss seeing the Prince fall, Tomi," said Archie.

"I thought you said no pig grease?" teased Nigel.

"On your mark!" Platt waited for Nigel and Archie to take their places.

On the sideline, one of the boys whispered in Corinna's ear. She nodded. When Platt said, "Go!" she jumped out and latched onto Nigel's leg. Archie took off running.

Her action briefly startled Nigel. "I thought you said cleanly!" Amused, Mirit picked up Corinna. Nigel set off running.

***

From their hiding place, Wyatt and Alyson watched the race. Alyson frowned. Wyatt laughed when Nigel purposely/accidentally pushed Archie into the creek.

"Hey! I haven't cheated!" Archie shouted.

"Who said you couldn't?" Nigel climbed a tree toward an apple. Two apples hung by a string on the branch.

Wyatt pointed at Nigel, who reached the top.

"I suppose he's funny. I want the boy to win," said Alyson.

Wyatt shrugged *why?*

"Just because," she groused with frustration.

They watched Archie retrieve an apple from the top and quickly follow Nigel down. Instead of reaching the bottom where Nigel waited for him, Archie leapt to one side nearest the bank. This put him ahead of Nigel.

"Hey!" shouted Nigel.

"You said I could cheat." Archie raced toward the finish line with Nigel hot on his heels. Archie may have been younger, but Nigel well trained. He soon overtook the boy, who grew winded from all the physical activity. Archie stumbled across the finish line just behind Nigel.

Wyatt enthusiastically clapped at Nigel's victory.

Alyson seized his hands. "Stop it! They'll hear us. We must be careful."

Timid, he shrunk back. "Sorry, Ally," he mumbled.

She hugged him. "So am I."

Wyatt tugged on Alyson's arm, as the soldiers moved to watch the victory celebration. He made a gesture between the table and his stomach.

"Ay, now would be a good time."

He dashed from the bushes toward the table. Unseen by Wyatt, Eli approached the table.

"Wyatt!" she called in a harsh warning whisper. Wyatt kept moving. He must not have heard. She darted behind a wagon used to transport the children. Her gaze nervously shifted between Eli and her brother.

Wyatt still didn't notice Eli, as he gleefully eyed the food trying to decide what to take first.

"You. Boy."

Wyatt didn't react, unaware that he was being spoken to. He stuffed bread into his mouth. He then took two apples and some cheese to put in each pocket of his jacket. His eyes grew wide with pleasure at seeing the venison meat pies. He just grabbed one when Eli questioned him.

"Why aren't you with the others?" His tone placid.

Fearful, Wyatt raced from the table. When he looked back at Eli, he ran into someone. The impact made him fall on his rump.

"What?" said a startled Mirit, the person he bumped into.

Terrified, Wyatt stared up at her. Eli approached. Wyatt scrambled to his feet only Mirit caught him.

"What are you afraid of?" she kindly asked.

For a moment, Wyatt tentatively regarded her, though not frightened.

"I asked him why he wasn't with others, but he ran from me," said Eli, innocently. "You shouldn't be scared by us," he told Wyatt.

Mirit focused on Wyatt. "Eli's right. We won't hurt you."

Wyatt held up the meat pie and motioned to his mouth.

She smiled. "They are good. Lady Magan made them."

Wyatt took a large bite. His eyes grew wide with delight. He vigorously nodded.

"Somebody sneaking food during the games?" teased Nigel. His arrival made Wyatt shy, only Mirit's hold prevented him from leaving.

"Apparently, he's very hungry," she said.

"Looks like it from the food he stuffed in his jacket." Nigel went to examine the jacket, which made Wyatt cringe.

Alyson intervened and knocked Nigel's arm away. "Leave my brother alone!"

"I wasn't hurting him."

Alyson stood defensively in front of Wyatt. Her glare defiant. Wyatt timidly peeked out from behind her.

"I didn't hurt you, did I?" asked Nigel.

Wyatt slowly shook his head.

"You were going to!" accused Alyson.

"No, I wasn't. What is your name?"

"Ally. Like a cat!" she declared then promptly kicked Nigel in the groin. She snatched Wyatt's hand and they ran off.

Nigel dropped to the ground in painful surprise. Mirit stood there uncertain whether to laugh or help him.

"Wait!" Eli's call prompted Virgil and Skylar to catch the children. They struggled to be loose from the Guardians.

"Let them go. They meant no harm," Mirit quickly said.

"Easy for you to say," groaned Nigel. He only rose to his knees, still in pain.

When released by the Guardians, Alyson and Wyatt took off again. He briefly looked back. She tugged on his arm to continue. Instead of joining the other children, they ran across the bridge into the orchard.

Platt, Chad, and Magan hurried over.

"What happened, Highness?" asked Platt.

Mirit helped Nigel to his feet where he gingerly tried to stand straight. "One little girl thought she was protecting her brother from Nigel. She did what all females do when they feel threatened," she explained with a suppressed snicker.

"I wasn't threatening her nor harming the boy," Nigel refuted.

"If you point them out to me, I will see they are disciplined," said Platt.

"That's not necessary," Mirit said to Nigel's chagrin.

"Excuse me?" Nigel huffed.

"She shouldn't be punished for acting in self-defense." Mirit's gaze swept over the children. Her brows furrowed with disappointment. "I don't see them."

Platt did a silent head count. "None appear to be missing."

"What?" Mirit looked again.

Nigel's gaze also scanned the faces. He flinched from time to time in discomfort. "They appeared to be twins, a boy and girl. Around ten or eleven years old with flaxen hair."

"I have no twins at the orphanage," said Platt.

"They ran into the orchard." Eli pointed in the direction Wyatt and Alyson fled.

Concerned, Chad called, "Dunsmore!" When the captain appeared, he said, "Search the orchard for a boy and a girl, twins, possibly orphans."

"Ay, my lord." Dunsmore summoned several soldiers to follow orders.

"No, they are frightened! Soldiers might scare them more," Mirit spoke in protest, only to be ignored.

"If they're not from the orphanage they could be in danger from Darnel," Chad told her.

"I'll go with them, Aunt Mirit," Eli volunteered.

"Avatar. Skylar." Mirit motioned them toward the orchard. "I hope they find them. He never said a word yet looked so frightened and vulnerable."

"She said enough," groused Nigel, then added with a hint of humor, "The last female who got physical with me, I married."

"Be serious. This is no joke!"

Nigel touched Mirit's shoulder in a gesture for calm. "I'm sorry," he softly whispered.

"It's getting dark, Princess. Time to take the children back," said Platt.

She curtly waved. "Go. I'll wait."

"Mirit. They will find the children," Nigel assured her. When she remained staunch, he spoke to Platt. "Do as she said, we'll wait."

Chad told Magan, "Take the boys home."

"Chad, you don't have to stay," said Mirit.

He kindly smiled. "I want to."

Three soldiers remained. They held torches for light. The rest helped gather the children for the return to Hagley.

"Mirit, does this have anything to do with last night?" Nigel privately asked.

"No!" she snapped; a bit louder than intended. She lowered her voice, but her tone still firm. "I don't want to arbitrarily fill the emptiness. However, I'm unsure if I can explain to your satisfaction. Something about him touched me deeply. Despite being very scared, he looked at me with vulnerability and trust." She battled against becoming emotional.

"That's a good enough explanation." He hugged her about the shoulders.

In the orchard, Alyson dodged through the trees. Wyatt occasionally looked back toward the commons. He tripped and fell. Something squished beneath him. He pushed up to his knees. One apple became smashed in the fall and mixed with the cheese. He licked his fingers and smiled with pleasure at the taste. His distraction was short lived when Alyson jerked him to his feet.

"Hurry! Or they'll catch us."

31

With a disagreeing grunt, he motioned back to the commons. "Her."

"No! We can't trust anyone. Now, come." She grabbed his arm, but he jerked away. "You want to get caught?"

He loudly sighed with indecision. Upon hearing pursuit, they ducked behind some bushes in an overgrown portion of the orchard. For several moments, they listened to sounds of soldiers searching around them.

"I don't see them, Captain," said one soldier.

"It's getting too dark to see anything," complained another.

"Ay," groused Dunsmore. "We need torches."

"Avatar, your sword," said Eli.

Alyson and Wyatt heard another language. Soon light illuminated the area. At first the they retreated into the shadows. Curious, Wyatt peeked through the bushes. Light radiated from Avatar's blade. Wyatt gasped in astonishment. He covered his mouth and ducked back.

"I think you may be right about it being too dark," began Avatar, though his voice sounded close to their hiding place. "My light can only reach so far for all of us to see. Captain, take your men back. Skylar and I can see just as well in the dark as in the light. All Guardians can," he said, sounding like he spoke directly to the bushes.

"I'm staying too," insisted Eli.

"If we leave, you'll have to tell the Princess why we couldn't find them," said Dunsmore.

"She will understand," said Eli.

"Princess?" Alyson mouthed to Wyatt.

They drifted back slightly when bright light flared then disappeared. For several moments, they listened to the sound of departing soldiers then all fell quiet. Wyatt began to relax. Hearing a gurgling sound from Ally, he reached into the pocket to give her some bread. She just took a bite when Skylar and Avatar appeared. Skylar from behind while Avatar in front.

"You can eat to your heart's content once we return," said Avatar.

She tried to scramble away but couldn't because of Skylar.

"We won't hurt you. We are Guardians, created by Jor'el to protect mortals," Avatar spoke with a reassuring voice.

32

Wyatt appeared apprehensive.

Eli arrived. "We sent the soldiers away, so they wouldn't frighten you."

Avatar gently turned Wyatt's face to look him directly in the eye. "You don't need to be afraid of me, Skylar or Eli."

"What about the Princess?" chided Alyson, not convinced.

"Mirit is the Princess who spoke to your brother. Nigel, the Prince, whom you took down. There are my aunt and uncle," said Eli kindly.

"Prince?" she repeated with fright.

"They sent us to find you," said Eli with reassurance.

Her defensiveness immediately returned. "To punish us?"

"No, to feed you." Avatar's bright silver eyes were kind and gentle in their regard. "Perhaps, even a bath and some new clothes. Now, come." She stiffened with apprehension when he took hold of her arm. "*Foise, beag cloinne*. Peace, little children," he spoke in the Ancient, while he held her gaze. She relaxed. He drew her from the brush while Skylar took charge of Wyatt.

They had only taken a few steps when Skylar went rigid with alarm. His hand gripped the hilt of his sword. At Wyatt's touch upon his arm, the Guardian forced a smile of reassurance.

"I think the quicker we get them to food the better," Skylar said to Avatar. Although he tried to maintain a level voice, his look conveyed his concern.

Avatar picked up Alyson.

"But—" she began to protest when he started running.

The Guardians kept a pace that Eli could manage at mortal full speed.

"Princess!" A soldier pointed.

Anxious, Mirit noticed Dunsmore and his men returned alone. "Captain, where are the children?"

"It's too dark for us to make an effective search even with Avatar's sword. The Guardians and the Prince are still searching."

33

"They won't stop until they are found," Nigel assured her.

"Highness, I think they did," said another soldier.

"Thank Jor'el," Mirit said in relief.

Eli breathed hard from running. He motioned to the Guardians carrying the children.

Mirit took little notice of Eli. Instead she focused on Alyson and Wyatt. "You shouldn't have run off. No one is going to hurt you." Wyatt appeared nervous and Alyson skeptical. Mirit smiled at Wyatt. "I see your pockets are still stuffed so you haven't eaten. You must be hungry. How would you will like some fresh food?"

He shrugged with uncertainty and looked to Alyson.

"What you do want from us?" she asked.

"Nothing. Only to help."

"Why?"

Mirit looked briefly stymied then said, "Because I can, and I feel I should. Will you let me help you?" Alyson didn't immediately answer, so Mirit turned to Wyatt. The boy lightly bit his lip. He looked with deliberation to Nigel, which prompted Mirit to say, "He wants to help too."

"*Humpf*," Alyson scoffed with disbelief.

"I do," began Nigel. "You won't know the truth of that unless you are willing to trust us."

"Adults can't be trusted!" She squirmed in Avatar's arm. "Put me down!"

He easily subdued her. With silver eyes steady upon her, Avatar calmly said, "You're wrong."

She stared back at him with confusion.

"Let us prove it," Nigel tried to encourage Alyson.

"Why should I trust you? Because you're a prince, and I'll be punished if I don't?" Despite her defensive tone, there was noticeable fear in her eyes.

Nigel spoke in gentle reply. "I may be a prince, but I'm not above Jor'el's law or duty to my station. It compels me to uphold divine law,

34

and the King's justice. Doubly so since I am The First Jor'ellian Knight of the Temple and the King's Champion."

Her brows furrowed. "That sounds important."

Nigel smiled at the innocent statement. "Ay. However, I think food is more necessary than an explanation. I hear hunger pangs."

Alyson glanced to Wyatt, who patted his stomach. She spoke to Nigel with guarded consent. "Very well. Prove it, Prince Knight."

Nigel heartily laughed. "Come, Ally cat, you'll ride with me." He took her from Avatar to place her on his horse.

"What is your name?" Mirit asked.

Wyatt balked with shy reluctance.

"Wyatt," said Alyson.

"Well, Wyatt, you will ride with me," said Mirit.

Skylar held his companions back. "This time I sensed a presence," he told Virgil.

Avatar grinned. "Mona. She arrived to check on the festivities.

"No, it wasn't her."

"Did you sense danger with the presence?" asked Virgil.

"No, but we don't want to take changes with our charges."

"Mona can do reconnaissance. I will summon her when all is settled for the night. Now, let us join them before Nigel grows suspicious of our lingering," said Avatar.

Chapter 4

ALYSON'S HOLD ON NIGEL WAS TENTATIVE AT FIRST. During the final steep climb from the city to the manor, she held on tightly so as not to fall off.

After entering the courtyard, Nigel drew the horse to rein. "You can let go now, we're here."

Alyson peeked out from behind him to view the manor. Torches and lamps illuminated the house. Skeptical, she asked, "You live here?"

"No, Sir Chad does." Nigel motioned to Avatar. The Guardian came to take Alyson down. He then dismounted.

Virgil helped Wyatt from Mirit's horse. The boy stared in awe at the manor.

"This is small compared to the palace where we live," Eli told Wyatt.

"Are you a prince too?" Alyson asked.

"Ay. My father is King," replied Eli.

Wide-eyed at the statement, Wyatt shook his head.

"There is nothing to fear," Mirit tried to reassure the children. "This manor, and our palace, are simply large homes where families live. Come." She took hold of Wyatt's hand. "You too." She held out a beckoning hand to Alyson.

Alyson hesitated. She accepted when Wyatt waved to her. Once inside, they met Magan.

"We have more guests, my dear," said Chad. "Wyatt and Ally. Twins." He introduced her to the children. "This is my wife, Lady Magan."

"Should we bow or something?" Alyson whispered with uncertainty to Wyatt.

Magan heard, and kindly smiled. "Welcome. I shall have rooms prepared."

"Rooms?" Fearful, Alyson seized Wyatt. "No, we stay together!"

"It's all right. You won't be separated," said Mirit.

"Of course not," agreed Magan. "One room, two beds, and two sets of nightclothes."

"Food first," said Nigel with a wink at Alyson. She began to smile only stopped, which increased his amusement.

"Come to the dining room while the room is prepared." Magan led the way.

Wyatt clung to Alyson's hand, as they passed from the foyer, through the grand hallway, and into the dining room. Both eyed the noble trappings of the manor with wonder and fascination.

"There is cider on the sideboard. It'll be a few moments for the food," said Magan

"Any meat pies left?" Mirit sent a nod and smile to the children.

Magan's expression showed understanding. "Two or three." She motioned for Chad to join her in leaving.

"Have a seat." Nigel escorted Alyson to the table. "Avatar will fetch the drinks."

"Who is Avatar?" she asked.

"I am, mistress." Avatar poured cider into the tankards. "He is Virgil, and that is Skylar." He placed a tankard in front of each of the twins, as they sat side by side.

"Mistress? I'm not a lady."

Wyatt chuckled into his tankard.

"She's named after a cat," teased Nigel. He took a seat opposite Alyson. He felt a warning poke in the ribs when Mirit sat beside him.

Alyson smirked at Nigel. "I'm named after my grandmother. Her name was Alyson."

"Alyson is a very pretty name. Much better than a cat. Do know what it means?" Nigel asked.

"No," she snorted at him then took a drink.

"It means *truthful.*"

She glanced at him from under furrowed brow of consideration. "What does your name mean?"

"Nigel has two meanings, born at night and Jor'el's blessing, which defines what happened. I was born at night, and my parents considered me a blessing from Jor'el."

Alyson shrank back in her chair to regard Nigel. Wyatt tugged on her arm, which diverted her marked attention. He pointed to himself with a shrug, to which she asked Nigel, "What does Wyatt mean?"

For a moment, Nigel regarded the boy. Despite not speaking, he outwardly appeared normal. "It means *defender.*"

Wyatt vigorously nodded, as he motioned between himself and Alyson.

"You defend your sister. That's good. I have two sisters I defend."

Wyatt held up two fingers with a curious smile.

"Ay, two." Nigel held up two fingers in response. "Eli is the son of one sister."

"Youngest son," added Eli. "I have two older brothers. And a sister about your age." He smiled at Wyatt.

Wyatt nodded with an understanding smile

"Why don't you speak?" asked Mirit.

The question made Wyatt recoil with a deep pouting frown.

"Please, I didn't mean to upset you. Was he born mute?" she asked Alyson.

The girl shook her head, a mindful, cautious glance to Wyatt. He snatched the tankard, only to find it empty. Avatar filled it with more cider.

Mirit changed back to the original subject. "Come to think of it, I don't recall what my name means."

Nigel took up the cue. "Mirit means *of the sea.*"

"That's fitting, since my father commands the navy."

"Our father was a sailor," droned Alyson.

The new piqued Mirit's interest. "Really? Are you from the West or East Coast?"

"West Coast."

Mirit balked but recovered quickly in an effort not to upset the children. "My father is Baron Mathias, lord of the West Coast."

Alyson shrugged with indifference. "Never heard of him."

"How did you come to be in the North Plains?"

"We were bought here."

"Bought?" echoed Nigel, with a slight edge of temper. He masked his irritation at another poke from Mirit. "What do you mean?" he asked in a more controlled tone.

"Food." Magan, Chad, and a servant arrived. All were unaware of interrupting the conversation.

This delayed a response since Alyson and Wyatt were eager to eat. Of primary interest to Wyatt, were the meat pies.

Magan ginned at the enthusiasm. "The room is ready, along with hot water, and servants to help with your bath."

Alyson swallowed hard in surprise while Wyatt paused in eating. "Bath?" she said.

"Of course," said Magan matter-of-factly.

"We bathe every day, though I only wash my hair once a week," said Mirit

Alyson grew thoughtful. "I can't remember the last time we took a bath."

"Cat's clean themselves every day," quipped Nigel.

"I don't have fur," Alyson shot back.

"No, just a swift kick. Ouch!" Nigel jerked in his seat. His head snapped around in surprise to Mirit, who kicked him under the table.

Wyatt laughed and pointed to Nigel. Alyson chuckled in agreement. "You're right, Wyatt, he is funny. I still wanted the boy to win," she said the last part to Nigel.

Mirit's quick grip on his arm kept Nigel from replying. Instead, she spoke to Alyson. "When you finish, I'll help you with the bath."

"Must we?"

"No, but the nightclothes are clean, along with a clean bed covered in soft silk sheets."

"Silk sheets?" Alyson repeated with awe. Wyatt gaped at the answer. They regarded their filthy, tattered clothes. Alyson asked in a sheepish tone, "A bath won't hurt, will it?"

Mirit chuckled. "No. And you will feel better."

Nothing more was said as the children finished eating. Magan and Mirit escorted the twins upstairs.

"You do have an unusual affect upon females, Highness," said Virgil wryly.

Nigel cocked a grin. "I wish I could figure out what is it about me that brings out their combative side. I understand sibling rivalry with my sisters, even why Mirit felt threatened when we first met. But Alyson? One statement and she fells me with kick."

"She said all adults are not to be trusted," Avatar said.

Nigel's brow knitted, pensive in consideration. "There is a harsh history behind those caustic words. Challenging me on being trustworthy is one thing, hearing her say they were bought ..." He couldn't finish for anger.

"She said that?" asked Chad, disturbed.

Nigel nodded, as he still tried to control his emotion. "She also mentioned their father was a sailor from the West Coast. That upset Mirit."

"You're hardly calm about it."

Nigel arched a brow at Chad. "Earlier I didn't understand what Mirit meant when she claimed the boy deeply touched her, now I do. Whatever happened to them has made her distrustful while he's withdrawn, for I don't believe he was born mute."

"Tomorrow we'll take them to Platt. He'll see they are well cared for," Chad offered with encouragement.

"If they survive the bath," said Virgil, smiling.

"Notice how I didn't go with them? Wet cats are all claws." Nigel used his hands to mimic an attacking feline.

Half an hour later, Mirit sat in one of the two chairs before a roaring fire in the hearth. Alyson sat on the footstool. Mirit used a towel to dry Alyson's hair. The girl wore fresh nightclothes under a dressing gown.

"That wasn't so bad, now was it?" asked Mirit.

"Well, it did hurt a bit to scrub my head and get tangles out of my hair."

A loud cry of exclamation came from the privy. Wyatt dashed out wet and naked. He headed for the chamber door. Nigel and Eli entered at the same time. Nigel caught Wyatt in the threshold.

"What's going on?"

"Here!" Mirit threw Nigel the towel she used. He wrapped it around Wyatt.

Ambrose hurried from the privy. The front of his apron, face and hair were very wet. "I'm sorry, Highness. He didn't like being … well, cleaned."

Nigel fought to suppress a laugh. "I understand." Feeling Wyatt shiver from the coolness of the autumn evening, Nigel steered him to the warm hearth to help him dry. "It took me a few times before I got used to being bathed by someone before I could do it myself," he said to Wyatt. The boy's lips quivered. "Where are his nightclothes?"

"In the privy," replied Ambrose.

"Thank you, Ambrose. I'll help him now." Nigel took Wyatt to the privy. Ambrose withdrew.

"Bring me another towel to finish Alyson's hair," said Mirit, to which she received an affirmative reply. She picked up a brush. "It's not good to sleep with wet hair. I'll brush it and use the warmth of the fire to help dry it before you retire."

"No one's brushed my hair since … I was younger."

"Not your mother?" Eli sat on a bench at the foot of the nearest bed.

"Grandmother. Our mother died the night we were born."

"I'm sorry."

Alyson shrugged. "They said grief at the news of father's death in a foreign war made her go into an early labor."

Stunned by the statement, Mirit paused in brushing.

41

"Why did you stop?"

Alyson's question along with Nigel and Wyatt's emergence from the privy, drew Mirit from her thunderstruck mood. Wyatt wore nightclothes, dressing gown and slippers. Nigel carried two towels. One he gave to Mirit. He caught her distressed glance. She returned to drying Alyson's hair with the towel. Nigel sat in the opposite chair. He patted the footstool for Wyatt.

"Sit here so I can dry your hair like Mirit is doing to Alyson."

"I like you brushing it," Alyson said.

"In a moment." Mirit watched a reluctant Wyatt.

Alyson frowned at his stubbornness. "Oh, Wyatt, sit down and let the prince knight dry your hair."

With a loud hump, Wyatt sat. He folded his arms in annoyance.

"Well, that's one way of getting him to cooperate," snickered Nigel.

Once Wyatt's sat, Mirit returned to brushing Alyson's hair, and continue the conversation. "You said your grandmother was the last person to brush your hair. How old were you then?"

"Seven."

"The grandmother you were named after?" asked Nigel.

"Ay." Alyson hissed at him like a cat.

"Glad I wasn't here for your bath," chuckled Nigel.

Wyatt jerked out from under the towel Nigel used to dry his hair. He pointed to Nigel and thumped his own chest.

"You wanted me here for your bath?" asked Nigel.

Wyatt made several agitated gestures, including some to the lower regions of his body. Alyson translated. "He didn't like the man Ambrose. Too rough in certain places."

Nigel swallowed back a laugh at the translation. "I'll see he doesn't help you again," he said to Wyatt.

Wyatt gave an officious nod. He pointed to his head, so Nigel went back to towel drying the boy's hair.

"When your grandmother brushed your hair at night, did she braid it or put it in a night cap?" asked Mirit.

"A night cap." Alyson grew somber in recollection. "I was wearing it the night they took us away."

"Took? Is your grandmother still alive?" asked Eli. He fought to mask distress during the conversation.

"No, she died. That's why they took us away to be bought."

Wyatt sniffled with distress. He wiped his nose.

"Was that recent?" asked Nigel.

"No!" Alyson bolted up. "I said I was seven last time she brushed my hair. Weren't you listening?"

"I'm sorry, I misunderstood," replied Nigel with sympathy. "Please, let Mirit finish with your hair while I tend to Wyatt. We'll speak no more about it tonight."

Mirit gently coaxed Alyson to sit. Nothing more was said until the children's hair was sufficiently dry. Wyatt yawned.

"Time for bed." Mirit escorted Alyson to one bed, while Nigel took Wyatt to the other.

"No! We stay together," said Alyson in distress. She clenched Wyatt's hand.

"You're in the same room," Mirit tried to soothe Alyson.

"I have an idea." Nigel went to the door and summoned the Guardians. "Virgil, move the nightstand from between the beds so Skylar can place them together."

Mirit guided the children to one side so the Guardians could follow instructions. Wyatt and Alyson watched in amazement as Virgil and Skylar moved the heavy, bulky furniture with ease.

"Is that better?" Nigel asked the twins. They nodded.

Once they were tucked into bed, Alyson asked, "What will happen to us tomorrow?"

"You'll have breakfast in the morning," said Mirit casually.

"Then we'll take you to Master Platt. He runs the orphanage," said Nigel matter-of-factly.

"Orphanage?" Alyson said with alarm. Wyatt gasped in terror.

Mirit quickly sat on the bed to calm them. "No, no orphanage! Nigel meant so he can speak with Master Platt to learn if there are any families in the area that want children. A lovely girl and handsome boy."

"What if there aren't any?" asked Alyson, still upset.

Mirit gently stroked the girl's cheek. "We'll take one day at a time. Now, sleep, and don't concern yourself about it."

Uneasy, Alyson glanced about the room. The low candlelight and fire made eerie, long shadows on the wall and ceiling. "We've never slept in a room like this before. Will you stay with us?"

"Until you fall sleep."

"Then we'll be alone?"

"No, I'll stay with you," Eli volunteered.

"So, will Virgil and Skylar." Nigel added when the twins appeared unconvinced. "Guardians were created by the Jor'el to protect mortals."

"Skylar has watched over me since I was born," said Eli. "His presence helped to keep away scary things in the night be they imaginary shadows." He made a hand puppet that reflected on the wall. Alyson flinched. Wyatt smiled. "Or safe from real danger until I became an adult."

"You're not an adult. Not like them," Alyson refuted in reference to Nigel and Mirit.

"I'm fourteen. I passed into adulthood last year, as is the custom when turning thirteen. Just like you will in a few years."

Nigel placed a hand on Eli's shoulder. "Granted, he's a young adult, but what he says is true about Guardians. They will be here all night to protect you. Mirit and I shall remain until you fall asleep."

Wyatt pointed to Virgil then placed his hands together by his head for the sign of sleep.

"No, we don't sleep. We are immortal and need neither sleep nor food."

"I saw you eating at the festival," said Alyson, confused.

"We can eat. Our bodies just don't require nourishment to stay alive."

Wyatt rubbed his stomach with a quizzical look.

"No, we don't suffer hunger either," said Skylar.

Wyatt rolled his eyes as if saying, '*wishful thinking*'.

"Now, you are safe and warm, so sleep peacefully." Mirit kissed Alyson on the forehead then did the same to Wyatt.

Skylar stood beside Alyson and Virgil near Wyatt. Skylar placed a gentle hand on Alyson's forehead. Virgil did the same with Wyatt. In unison, they spoke the Ancient: "Sleep in Jor'el's peace." Within a moment, the children fell asleep.

After an affirming nod from Skylar, Nigel drew Eli aside. "With Skylar and Virgil here, you don't need to stay."

Concerned compassion made Eli glance to the bed. "I want to stay. In fact, I believe I should stay."

"Very well." While Nigel turned to leave, Mirit hesitated. "Mirit?"

She didn't answer him. Instead, she spoke quietly to Eli. "Fetch me if they stir."

"I will. Goodnight, Aunt." He tenderly kissed her cheek.

Nigel gently drew Mirit from the children's room to their chamber. Since discovery of the twins, she acted in ways he had not seen in years: anxious and distressed. Several times she poked or jabbed him while at other times verbally defensive. He suspected the cause, yet would she admit it?

"Mirit, about Platt and the orphanage—" he couldn't finish as her passion came forth in quick reply.

"I had to say something to calm their fear! I couldn't let them lie awake all night wondering what will happen."

"I understand. Yet, you know Platt is a good man. He can find them a home."

"How long will that take? It's already been four years since they've known the love and stability of home and family. You see what it's done to them. I don't want them put in the orphanage!"

He tried to calm her. "I wasn't going to do that. I meant to introduce them to Platt since he doesn't know them. Also, to learn if he's heard of anyone buying or selling children in the province." He took her hand. A soft smile appeared, as he gazed at her. "Remember, I also have a soft spot for orphans."

She sighed with frustration. "Nigel, it's more than that."

"Obviously. What did Alyson say to upset you?"

She gathered her emotions before replying. "You know how old they are, correct?"

"Ay, eleven."

"That is what me struck me so hard."

"Their age?" he asked, confused.

"No, no! Their father was a sailor, and their mother died from an early labor caused by grief at the news of his death in a *foreign* war." He still appeared confused, so she hurried to continue. "Nigel, the only foreign war around the time of their birth was Tunlund! They are from the West Coast, meaning he served in my father's fleet that came to rescue Titus and me."

The news visibly struck him with sudden understanding. He tenderly kissed her hands. "Mirit, you're not responsible for what happened to their parents."

"I realize that, but don't you see the connection?"

"It is a disturbing coincidence to be sure."

"A Jor'ellian speaking of coincidence?" she chided.

"You know what I mean—"

She pulled away from him. "How long are we to stay, two, three weeks perhaps?"

"Ay, around that time length."

"Then as long as we are here, I want them with us."

"Mirit—"

She rushed to interrupt. "Platt can look for a family during that time, but don't put them in the orphanage!" her voice cracked with emotion. She fought back tears.

Nigel held her. "Very well. I'm certain Chad and Magan won't object to two more guests." He tenderly brushed away her tears. "My only concern is what will happen if Platt does find them a home."

"They'll finally be happy."

He took her face in his hands. "I mean, how will you feel?"

"I just want them in a place where Alyson won't feel compelled to fight, and Wyatt can find his voice again."

"I want the same." He began to snicker under his breath.

"It's not funny!"

"Since Ambrose had difficulty with Wyatt, a sudden image came to mind of Alyson acting like a wet cat." He did a feline hiss, using his hand as a claw.

She lightly laughed. "Actually, she did better than I expected. And you shouldn't tease her so cruelly."

"I didn't think I was being cruel. However, I wonder what it is about my manner that makes *certain* women combative." He flashed a sardonic grin and tweaked her nose.

"Perhaps it is your charming arrogance, prince knight." She playfully jabbed him in the midsection, which made him take an impulsive and protective step back. She laughed. "Alyson said you probably look like a drowned rat in a bath, and one a cat would pounce on and devour."

"You say I'm cruel?"

She took his face in her hands. She lovingly smiled. "To me you're an adorable drowned rat."

Chapter 5

L ATER IN THE NIGHT, AVATAR ENTERED THE BEDCHAMBER. Skylar and Virgil stood on either side of the adjoining beds. Eli sat in a large cushioned chair beside the hearth. He fought a yawn as he read a book.

Quizzical at Avatar's arrival, Eli rose to meet the Guardian. "Is something wrong?" he asked in a hushed tone.

"No, Highness. I simply wanted to check on the children."

"They haven't stirred since falling asleep."

Avatar's gaze went to Skylar and Virgil. He made the merest of nod to them before saying to Eli, "If I may, I need to speak with Skylar and Virgil for a few moments."

"I thought you said nothing is wrong?"

"Guardian business," Avatar kept his voice neutral. "We won't be long."

In passing to leave, Skylar whispered to Eli. "Remember, we put them to sleep. They won't wake before morning."

"I'll sit by the bed to make certain." Eli moved a small chair beside the bed on Alyson's side.

Being a frequent visitor to Hagley, Avatar knew the manor well. He led Virgil and Skylar to a guest salon at the end of the hall. The room was dark with no lamps and the curtains closed. Avatar whispered a few words in the Ancient. The lamp gave off dim light. Just enough for visibility, but not enough to be seen under the door.

Avatar closed his eyes to stretch out his senses; the common way to connect with other Guardians. It took several moments before he opened his eyes.

White light of dimension travel appeared. Mona emerged from the faded light. She stood six inches shorter than the warriors at seven-feet tall. Long brown hair accented her bright aquamarine eyes. Her vassal uniform reflected her station as Trio Leader of the North Plains. The knee-length form-fitting jacket showed feminine tailoring. The pants were cut to look like a skirt more than manly trousers. She wore a dagger on the belt. She noticed Virgil and Skylar before addressing Avatar.

"What brings you to the North Plains, Commander? Visiting your former captain?"

"Something like that. Nigel and Mirit are here also."

"Ah. This is an official visit."

"No, a holiday. However, something occurred today, which requires your help. At separate times throughout the day, Virgil and Skylar sensed a presence. One that can cause trouble, *if* it exists."

"How can we sense a presence that doesn't exist?" chided Virgil.

Avatar ignored Virgil and continued to Mona. "Summon your Trio Mates."

Mona mimicked Avatar's earlier posture with closed eyes to stretch out for a summons. Brighter light filled the room when the Trio Mates appeared together. Dale, a lanky female ranger, wore the customary uniform of forest colors. Autumn gold hair reached her shoulders. Jade eyes viewed everything with skepticism. Like all rangers, she carried a quarterstaff and dagger. Kendra wore the muted colored robe of her scholarly station with ankle length skirt, and no weapons. Her hair fell in long ringlets of black. Her pale lavender eyes gleamed with keen intellect.

"You summoned us?" asked Kendra.

Dale irreverently smirked. "We have visitors." She indicated the warriors to Kendra.

"Prince Nigel, Princess Mirit, and Prince Eli are here," Mona informed her Trio Mates.

"So that's what brings the infamous Commander our way," Dale taunted Avatar.

"More to see if your attitude has improved before inflicting your presence upon their Highnesses," he rebuffed.

Mona quickly intervened before Dale could reply. "There may be trouble, which is why *Commander* Avatar requested I summon you. To investigate a possible threat." She stressed his rank to Dale.

The ranger warily regarded Avatar. "What trouble?"

"At different times during an outing with the orphans, Virgil and Skylar sensed a presence."

"Nothing specific, yet unusual, and concerning," said Skylar.

"You can't tell us anymore than that? Just a sense?" asked Dale.

"Are you questioning my sense of caution concerning my charges' welfare?" demanded Virgil.

"A possible threat, if it even exists."

Avatar's quick, strong hand on Virgil's shoulder stopped a reply to Dale's ridicule. Instead, Avatar spoke in a nonchalant tone. "We are detained by our duties, and don't want to arouse suspicion or alarm, should it be proven a mistake."

"A mistake? A warrior admitting to a mistake?"

"Dale!" said Mona in warning.

"Possible mistake. And it would be Virgil's mistake not mine."

Dale huffed a chuckle. "I'll try to remember the distinction, Commander."

Hearing Virgil's growl of annoyance, Avatar's restraint visibly increased.

Kendra's astute gaze shifted between the warriors. "Was this sense strong enough to effect two Guardians at once?"

"Separate incidences. Virgil sensed it before the festivities, and Skylar afterwards. Something may be stirring. The question of *what* needs to be discovered."

"The mortal Darnel is here. I wonder if that is who was sensed," continued Kendra.

Dale distastefully sneered. "He is an irritant boil that needs to be lanced."

"We can't force him to leave," Kendra scolded the ranger.

"Who said force? Just make it so unpleasant that he chooses to depart. Perhaps bitter water. Just say the word." Dale tapped her staff.

"Subtlety will work better than foul water."

"How so, scholar? Find a loophole in the law?"

"It worked in keeping him from entering Hagley, didn't it?" said Kendra with a triumphant grin.

"Ay," came Dale's mumbled agreement.

"Your mission," Avatar loudly interrupted the argument, "is to track down the sense, not deal with Darnel, no matter how obnoxious a mortal he may be."

"I still say he's more of a real threat than any phantom sense." Dale's eyes darted to Virgil and Skylar.

Virgil's reply came low and menacing. Icy blue eyes narrowed upon her. "Ranger, you are trying my patience."

"Any time, warrior," Dale brashly returned.

Mona and Kendra seized Dale to keep her from further provocation when Virgil gripped the hilt of his sword.

"We'll begin by securing Hagley," Mona said to Avatar.

"Discreetly," he cautioned.

"Females are always discreet."

"Even one as bombastic as Dale?" chided Virgil.

Mona laughed. "You have me there." Before Dale could refute, the females disappeared without stepping back from the warriors. The brilliance temporarily blinded them.

"I hope being demeaned and blinded is worth it," Virgil complained. He rubbed his eyes in recovery.

Avatar also blinked to refocus. "Unfortunately, it's worse. I thought it was just me. However, Dale's vicious attack of you two, and suggesting action against a mortal, is troubling."

Suddenly suspicious, Skylar spoke. "Wait! You purposely used us to provoke her? Why?"

"Because I needed a genuine reaction not enforced tolerance."

The answer confused Skylar. "How does making us ranger bait change what you asked them to investigate?"

"It doesn't. We need to know the source of the danger." Avatar's brow leveled in consideration.

Virgil's expression shifted to immediate annoyed comprehension. "You didn't come here for a casual visit. Everything said just now shows you already knew." He motioned between himself and Skylar. "We didn't sense phantoms, did we?"

Avatar sent Virgil a reproving glare. "Has anyone mentioned, you're as irritating as Dale?"

The rebuff didn't faze Virgil. Instead, it infuriated him. "What haven't you told us?"

"Return to the children," Avatar roughly dismissed them.

Virgil stiffened. "We have a right to know if it will endanger our charges!"

"I said return to duty. That's an order."

Skylar grabbed Virgil. "The Commander has spoken."

Virgil shook off Skylar to march from the room. Skylar's own vexation came out. "I hope whatever the reason, it's worth the risk of keeping us ignorant."

Avatar didn't reply, rather made a curt motion of his head for Skylar to leave.

<hr />

At the campsite, Darnel, his wife Sophia, eldest son Vance, wife, Genna, and youngest son Colby, gathered around the fire to eat. Being ten years apart, the brothers didn't look much alike. Vance resembled his father. Colby took after his mother with lighter hair and smooth skin, not capable of growing any substantial beard.

The appearance of a very tall, cloaked and hooded figure startled them. The figure held a shielding medal.

Darnel scowled after he recovered from the brief fright. "I wish you wouldn't do that."

The figure didn't reply, rather stared at Darnel. He grew uncomfortable at light eyes peering out from under the hood.

"No, I haven't found them yet. I believe they are here. Or at least, came this way.

The being's voice sounded in a lower, unnatural register. "Your presence is causing disruption."

"I thought finding them was paramount?" said Darnel, a bit confused.

"To you, not me. Discovery of your misuse of the law to shield your enterprise would not set well with the King."

"Why would you betray us? We've done everything you asked."

"Continuation is more important than the instrument used in the process. Keep that in mind. Now, act quickly!" The figure donned the shielding medal and disappeared.

"Do you think—," Colby became silenced by a sharp hand from his father.

Darnel warily looked about. "The Guardian maybe still here, or least close enough to hear." He shoved his empty plate into the wife's hand. "Come morning, you two will find a way into Hagley to make a search, and contact our compatriot," he said to his sons.

Avatar remained in the room. Twenty minutes passed since he dismissed Virgil and Skylar. Whereas he participated in clandestine activities before, it went against the grain to act gruff with fellow Guardians, especially a close comrade.

Virgil replaced him as Guardian Overseer to Nigel. Well, actually, Virgil became keenly astute to Mirit, and a bond formed during the trip to Natan. Still, it proved difficult to yield the position to another after nearly thirty-five years. Being terse with Virgil troubled Avatar since Virgil had every right to be concerned. However, orders for strict secrecy called for unusual behavior.

Avatar became braced when a dimmed light appeared. It Mona returned.

"The watch is set, and the plan in motion," she said.

He simply nodded. His brows drawn low.

53

"Something wrong?" she asked at his brooding silence.

"Ask me when this over."

"Is it because of earlier?"

His expression turned resolute. "I'll say this, at the slightest hint of threat to the mortals, I will act."

Unperturbed, she replied calmly. "None of us will let that happen. No scenario has been missed. At least, on our part."

"I thought so in the past only to be proven wrong." Avatar left.

In the hall, he paused at the door to the children's apartment. Mona tried to encourage him, but such a harsh response from Virgil was something he didn't expect. The plan couldn't continue with such tension.

Upon entering, he noticed Virgil stiffen. Eli had fallen asleep in the chair. Skylar stood in his usual stoic manner. With a curt hand gesture, Avatar signaled Virgil from the room.

Once away from the door, Avatar took a deep breath followed by a long exhale to release earlier anger. He kept his voice neutral. "You realize I don't owe you an explanation?"

"Ay. But if it poses a danger—"

Avatar's raised hand stopped Virgil. His eyes focused directly on his friend. "Do you trust me?"

The question briefly stymied Virgil. "What does that have to do with this?"

Avatar lowered his voice but remained firm. "Nigel was my charge since birth. Mirit, for a few years, but Tunlund made as strong a bond between us, as Natan did for you and her. I would do nothing to expose them to danger."

Truth of the statement drained Virgil of any lingering annoyance. He glanced down the hall to the room where Nigel and Mirit slept. "I take it you're under orders."

"From Kell and Tyrone."

Hearing the double confirmation made Virgil clasp the hilt of his sword ready for duty. "I wish you had told me this before. I never would have let my temper get the best of me."

"I shouldn't have to tell you anything past giving you an order—if your trust in me was complete."

Cut to the quick, Virgil gaped. "I … I didn't mean … I'm just concerned." He motioned down the hall. "I'm truly sorry, Avatar." In shame, he looked at his feet. A hand on his shoulder made him tentatively raise his head.

"I did the same with Kell on a number of occasions when I thought trouble could impact Nigel. He tolerated my insubordination. Virgil, I don't want tension between us, not just for their sake. We both know what hostility did to our ranks."

"I would never take it that far! Centuries of Soren imprisonment showed me the importance of friendship and loyalty."

"Then I ask for your unquestioning support."

Again, Virgil gripped his sword. "You have it, Commander." He flashed a wry smile. "I suppose if you can serve as a verbal practice target for an archer, I can endure being ranger bait."

Avatar fought to keep his mirth to a low chuckle. "I won't tell Wren you said that. She might add a second warrior to her target list." He nudged Virgil. "Return to duty."

Chapter 6

WYATT WOKE THE NEXT MORNING SURPRISED TO SEE VIRGIL beside the bed. He relaxed when the Guardian smiled.

"Good morning, young master."

Wyatt grinned. He felt a stirring beside him. Alyson moved yet remained asleep. Wyatt made a quiet sign to Virgil before carefully climbed out of bed. Virgil handed him a dressing gown. He put on his slippers. He headed for the privy when he noticed Skylar sitting on the floor with his eyes closed. He quizzically glanced to Virgil, pointed to Skylar, and made the sign for sleep.

Virgil approached Wyatt to quietly reply. "No, he's not asleep. Guardians meditate to rest, though we don't really need rest either."

"And become instantly awake and alert." Skylar's voice briefly startled Wyatt.

"Mortals do need rest," said Eli. He yawned and stretched from his place on the sofa. "Did you sleep well?"

Wyatt nodded.

Alyson awoke.

"Good morning, mistress," greeted Virgil.

"I'm not a mistress."

Virgil just smiled. He held another dressing gown when she tossed aside the covers to rise.

"That's how Guardians address all mortals," said Eli.

Alyson looked surprised to see Eli. "Did you stay here all night also?"

Eli nodded, since he attempted to stop a yawn.

"Why?"

"Because I didn't want you to wake in a strange place and be afraid."

56

Alyson bit her lip at the answer. She felt Virgil gently touch her shoulder.

"You'll find clean clothes on the couch in the dressing area. After breakfast, Princess Mirit will take you both shopping," said Virgil

"Shopping for what?"

"New clothes, of course. Shoes, maybe a slight haircut." Virgil examined her damaged hair. "You need a trim, and some ointments to restore the health and shine."

"Guardians know about such things?"

Skylar and Virgil laughed. Virgil replied, "We've learned many things from observing, and interacting with mortals for many centuries."

Alyson gaped at them. Wyatt tugged on her arm, also astonished. He pointed to Virgil and Skylar. She asked the question, "How old are you?"

"Over fourteen hundred years. Skylar is around sixteen hundred. Avatar is the oldest at eighteen hundred. We are created to be immortal."

At the twins' thunderstruck expression, Eli said, "I gather you haven't encountered Guardians before."

Wyatt shook his head.

"Only heard about them. We've never seen any until yesterday," said Alyson.

Wyatt's brow suddenly furrowed, which prompted Eli to ask, "Is something wrong?"

The boy hurried to the privy, much to Eli's amusement, and Alyson's annoyance.

"Don't take too long! I have to go too," she called.

Once finished in the privy, Alyson and Wyatt dressed. To her surprise, Virgil knew how to brush hair. He also did a very good job braiding then pinning it up. She admired herself in the mirror.

"I've never worn my hair like this before. Where did you learn to do it?"

"Princess Mirit. Sometimes we would be on assignment away from Waldron or the Fortress, and I helped her to be presentable for a diplomatic task. After all she is the Queen's Champion."

Alyson turned from the mirror to ask, "What's that?"

"Counterpart to uncle, who is the King's Champion," replied Eli. "Both are trained in combat for defense of the King and Allon." He helped Wyatt finish dressing.

Curious, Wyatt pointed on Virgil's sword.

"Ay, the Princess fights very well. In fact, they practice every day before breakfast. I usually participate, but today, my task is to look after you and Mistress Alyson."

"Uncle taught me how to fight," said Eli.

"I taught Nigel, in his youth." Avatar entered unnoticed.

Wyatt motioned between himself and Avatar. He pretended to grip a sword.

Avatar flashed an agreeable grin. "I could teach you, but why don't we go see them at practice before eating."

Wyatt widely smiled with eagerness.

Alyson shrugged. "I suppose it could be fun to see the prince knight at work."

❦

When the twins and Guardians arrived at the armory, Dunsmore and Chad joined Mirit and Nigel in daily exercise. It was certainly different seeing them dressed in breeches, shirt, and practice gear instead of fine clothes. Mirit's hair was starkly pulled back in a tight braid that knotted on her head; similar to what Virgil did with Alyson's hair.

For several moments, the twins watched Dunsmore spar with Nigel while Chad engaged Mirit. The clang of swords echoed in the chamber. These were vigorous bouts that tested each combatant.

Wyatt seized Avatar's arm. He pointed and grunted with enthusiastic glee. Virgil noticed Alyson seemed impressed. When she caught him looking at her, she tried to hide it with pretended indifference. At the end of the bouts, Wyatt loudly clapped. This drew the attention to their presence.

"We have an audience," snickered Nigel. He accepted a towel from Dunsmore to wipe the sweat from his face.

"Good morning, you two. Sleep well?" asked Mirit.

58

"Ay," said Alyson. She assumed a nonchalant posture when Nigel approached.

With animated interest, Wyatt motioned between Mirit and Nigel then to himself. He surprised everyone by trying to speak, but only managed "Def—".

"Defend?" asked Nigel.

Wyatt vigorously nodded. He took hold of Alyson's arm.

Nigel smiled. "Ay. I can teach how to defend your sister."

Alyson became disturbed at the exchange.

"What of you, Alyson? Would like to learn?" asked Mirit.

The girl replied with indignation. "I have been defending him!" When Wyatt gave her a pleading, apologetic look, she ran from the armory.

"Alyson!" called Nigel.

"No, let me. I believe I know what's wrong." Mirit handed her sword to Chad before she hurried after Alyson.

There weren't many places to go in the courtyard with the main gate closed. Frustrated, Alyson raced to the far side of the house to another smaller gate. Mirit caught her.

"Let go!" Alyson protested.

Mirit wouldn't yield. "Stop fighting. Yourself, and me." She pinned the girl against the wall. "I understand!"

"How could you? You're not an orphan."

"I understand the feeling of having to fight everything and everyone all the time. To lash out and strike before someone or something hurts you. I transferred that impulse to the sword, and once made my living by fighting to entertain."

"You're a princess," refuted Alyson, though less combative.

"By marriage." Mirit tenderly caressed Alyson's face. "I see some of my youthful tendencies in the way you defend Wyatt and are sarcastic with Nigel. He and I fought like a cat and dog when we first met."

The statement intrigued Alyson. "Really?"

"Ay. When the situation became dangerous, he protected me even though all I did was wound him with harsh words. I couldn't admit I was afraid. That's what you've done, protect Wyatt because he's afraid."

Alyson became upset to the point of tears. "He wants to defend me, but he doesn't remember what happened last time!"

"What did happen?" When Alyson grew conflicted and hesitant, Mirit held her face. She spoke with tender imploring, "Please, tell me."

Tears began even before Alyson told the tale. "Wyatt tried to protect me from him, but he became angry, and nearly beat Wyatt to death! He didn't wake up for a week. He couldn't talk or remember anything." She sobbed hard.

Mirit held Alyson. She fought back her own tears of sympathy. "You fear the same will happen again if he defends you." She felt Alyson nod. "How old were you then?"

Alyson replied between efforts to control her emotions. "Nine. When Wyatt was well enough, we ran away."

Mirit lifted Alyson's head to look at her. "You've been on the run ever since?"

"We keep moving, hoping he won't find us." She swallowed back a sob. "I don't want my brother hurt anymore. He's just starting to talk, at least a few words."

Mirit gently wiped the tears from Alyson's face. "We won't let anyone hurt either of you."

"Wyatt wants the prince knight and old Guardian to teach him to fight!"

Mirit fought to hide a smile at an age reference she assumed to be Avatar. She led Alyson to sit on a nearby bench. "It's natural for a brother to defend his sister. It shows how much he loves you. Although he may not remember, he knows you have shouldered the burden for so long. Don't be angry with Wyatt, or fear for him. Nigel and Avatar are excellent fighters. What they teach Wyatt, will benefit him, not solely in defense, but more so in confidence, courage and respect. The attributes of a Jor'ellian."

Alyson sniffled. "What's a Jor'ellian?"

"A knight dedicated to Jor'el, the Almighty."

"I've heard of Jor'el, but not always good. He didn't like Jor'el."

"He who?"

"The one who bought us and beat Wyatt!"

"Does he have a name?"

Alyson shrugged, unwilling to reply.

"Very well, you don't have to tell me." Mirit again lifted Alyson's head to look at her. "I don't want you to be afraid for Wyatt, or for yourself. When I stopped being afraid, it allowed me to return Nigel's affection. I discovered a kind, generous, and loving man. You too can discover a better life when you let go of fear."

"How long ago was that?"

"Eleven years. Your entire life."

"You've been happy ever since?"

"Ay."

"What about your children, are they happy too?"

Mirit flinched slightly at the question. "We don't have any children. I'm not capable of bearing any."

"That troubles you?"

Mirit kindly smiled. "It's probably difficult for you to understand right now, but when you love someone deeply, and you can't give him the greatest gift a woman can, it's hard to accept at times. You begin to regret the inability."

"Is that why you brought us here? Because of your regret?"

Hearing the girl's skepticism return, Mirit quickly said, "No! I told you before, I want to help. We've been helping orphans for years. You heard Chad tell how he met Nigel when he was eight. We may not have children of our own, but we have ten nieces and nephews ranging in age from three years to eighteen. Eli is one of them. Not to mention being godparents of Chad and Magan's sons. Children are a large part of our lives. So," she said with soft, prompting smile, "for however long it takes to search for your new family, let us enjoy the time together."

Wyatt rushed over with Nigel and Eli close behind. The boy looked distressed. "Al … lee?"

"I'm fine."

Nigel attempted to bring levity to the situation. "Talking behind our backs, eh?"

"And if we were? What would you do, prince knight?" Alyson tossed a smile at Mirit.

"Take your brother to breakfast and fill his ears with stories of how to straighten out wayward females."

Alyson gasped at Nigel's retort, which made Wyatt laugh. For Alyson's sake, Eli bit back his amusement.

Mirit sent a brief scowl to Nigel. She grinned when Alyson turned to her. "Breakfast sounds like a good idea." She took Alyson by the arm. "Then Nigel and I need to bathe and change before going into town to take you shopping."

"Good idea, Aunt Mirit," said Eli.

Mirit regarded Eli's wrinkled state. "I gathered you remained with them all night."

"Ay." He fought a yawn. "Food and a bath will wake me up."

<hr>

After breakfast, and a quick bath, Eli called upon his aunt and uncle. Mirit sat at the vanity to fix her hair while Nigel dressed. She saw his arrival via the mirror.

"Eli, were there any problems last night?"

"No, they slept soundly." He plopped in a chair beside the vanity. He fought a yawn.

Mirit cocked a smile. "You didn't sleep well."

"A chair is not the most comfortable, but I managed a couple of hours," he tried to pass it off with a casual reply.

She took hold of Eli's hand. "It was very sweet of you to remain with them."

Eli leaned forward to speak seriously. "I sense what you did, that there is something deeply touching about them. I'm not sure what, but I felt compelled to stay."

Mirit gently touched his cheek. "Compassion for others is one of your most endearing qualities."

Eli scowled, as he sat back. "I sometimes wonder if it is a weakness."

"Don't ever think that."

"Mirit's right." Nigel stood in front of a full-length wardrobe mirror to finish buttoning his doublet. "Compassion is needed to counter resolve when it comes to justice."

"It kept me from fighting," Eli grumbled with annoyance.

Nigel and Mirit exchanged glances of comprehension. Nigel moved to Eli. "Do you resent your mother sending you to protect the other children rather than engage in battle?"

"Not resent exactly. I can fight!" he insisted.

"No one has ever doubted that. Yet, understand, when it comes to the defense of the family, and Allon, we each must utilize our strengths. Titus will someday take the throne. Fraser is studying to become a Jor'ellian Knight. You—"

"Have no real function."

"That's not true!" Nigel drew Eli to stand to look him straight in the eye. "I didn't get to be First Jor'ellian based solely on my combat skills. Diligent following of Jor'el's principles, and faith, played important parts. Never underestimate faith and dedication. Often, they accomplish more than a sword. Your faith and compassion undergird others. *That* is why Tristine sent *you* as their protector."

"Eli," began Mirit with encouragement. "What does your heart say? To do battle or to help in whatever way you can?"

For a moment, Eli stared at Mirit. "To help."

"Then follow your heart, because those desires are placed there by Jor'el. And no one questions that."

A quick smile or relief crossed Eli's lips. "I didn't come to talk about me. I wanted to know what upset Alyson."

"A good question. We haven't discussed it either," said Nigel.

Mirit briefly pressed her lips together in consideration of her reply. "Wyatt's desire to learn to protect her brought back bad memories of the last time he did so." Her voice became woeful. "His muted condition is the result of a vicious beating that happened two years ago when he tried to protect her from their owner. It took a week before he woke up. He couldn't speak or remember what happened. They've been on the run ever since."

Nigel's jowls flexed with rage. "How could a man so beat a boy as to cause him such injury?"

"According to Alyson, one who doesn't think much of Jor'el."

"Did she name him?" asked Eli in a strained voice of anger.

Mirit solemn shook her head. "It's too painful."

"He will fear Jor'el, and royal justice, when I find out who he is!" declared Nigel.

Mirit quickly stood. "Though your feelings are justified, the children don't need to see any more anger. What they need is gentle handling and kind words. Exactly what you told Eli."

Nigel sarcastically grinned. "She's so much like you were when we first met."

"You're changing the subject."

Nigel kissed her hand. "No, because of our past, I understand. They won't see anger from me."

Eli fought his emotions. "Why should that stop Wyatt from learning to defend her?"

"She fears it could happen again," replied Mirit. "I told her that accepting instruction from Nigel and the *old Guardian* will greatly benefit Wyatt." She curbed a smile

"Old Guardian?" Nigel questioned with snicker.

Eli smiled. "Virgil told their ages when Alyson asked how long Guardians live and cited who was the eldest."

Nigel heartily laughed. "Oh, Avatar will love hearing that." He calmed down to return to the subject at hand. "You do remember I want to speak with Platt?" he asked Mirit.

"Ay. Only you won't worm your way out of shopping, like other times." When he feigned ignorance, she added, "Don't pretend. True, Daria and Mikela are a chatty duo. Yet, I believe Alyson needs you to be there."

The statement baffled Nigel. "Why?"

"You are right about our similarities. I needed your approval when we first married to help rebuild my life. I don't know what Wyatt protected her from, be it physical abuse or male baseness, but she needs to see the kinder, gentler side of a man. Just like you act with your nieces."

It a moment of consideration before Nigel said, "I offer a compromise, since it is important I speak with Platt. Chad, Avatar, and I will inconspicuously make a jaunt to the orphanage without their knowledge then meet you for luncheon to spend the rest of afternoon at your disposal."

She frowned. "You won't yield about Platt, will you?"

"You know it must be done. I will put hard questions to him about finding them a good, safe, and loving home. One that meets with our approval."

"They will notice your absence."

"Tell them I have a surprise."

"You mean lie?" she challenged him.

"No. I will have a surprise when I join you."

Mirit remained skeptical. "Very well. After this, no more sidestepping female matters when you are needed." She waved a finger in his face.

"Now who's pretending? You can't *tolerate* it either. You merely indulge our nieces to keep the family peace."

When she flushed with embarrassment, Eli winked, and said, "I'll pretend I didn't hear that."

Chapter 7

ALYSON AND WYATT TRIED TO HIDE THEIR CURIOSITY, AS THEY rode in a carriage down to the city. Mirit, Eli, and Magan accompanied the children. Virgil sat with the driver. Skylar walked behind the carriage. Nigel and Chad rode horses with Avatar accompanying them.

At the appointed place, Nigel, Chad, and Avatar deviated from the path in such a manner as to go undetected by young eyes. Deception was not the intent, merely a means to avoid upsetting the children unnecessarily.

Chad led Nigel and Avatar to the orphanage's rear entrance. They went to Platt's office located on the first floor with visibility to the main street and the inner courtyard. A modest, comfortable room, complete with books and ledgers. Platt willingly allowed access to the records.

For an hour, Nigel sat at Platt's desk. Chad occupied a large cushioned chair by the window to read. Avatar stood beside a bookshelf. All were immersed in viewing the material Platt provided.

"Everything appears to be in order," said Nigel. "You can record the adoption of Archie to Captain Dunsmore." He handed Platt the paper he signed and sealed with his signet ring.

"Thank you, Highness." Platt offered them refreshment. Nigel and Chad accepted the cider while Avatar declined.

The Guardian crossed to the desk with a ledger in hand. "There is something I noticed. Over the last four years two families have repeatedly adopted orphans." He placed the book on the desk in front of Nigel. "A farmer by the name of Moreland, and Ike, the butcher. It appears Ike showed an interest in Archie." He indicated the entries over several pages.

"Archie?" Nigel scanned the indicated page. "Ike wanted to adopt him, why?" he asked Platt.

"He's been apprenticed to Ike for the past year. When boys are old enough, I send them to learn a trade. It's often the best way for them to be adopted."

"That's why you kept him and Dunsmore apart," chided Chad.

"No, my lord. Adoptions are usually to families, not single individuals."

"It took much convincing for you to allow Dunsmore to adopt Archie."

"I have nothing against the captain, my lord. My concerns are for the children."

Nigel raised both hands for the argument to cease. "The point is moot since Archie is happy with his adopted father. And I know Dunsmore's quality as a man and soldier."

"Agreed, Highness. Also, I can assure you, Moreland and Ike provide loving homes."

Avatar raised a skeptical eyebrow. "Seven children for a butcher? The farmer I could see having eight, especially if his holdings are large."

His interest piqued by the observation; Nigel examined other entries Avatar indicated. "Is the butcher and his wife childless that they continue to adopt?"

"No, they have three of their own. One moved to Rockland to start his own butcher shop."

"Archie would have made eleven. An unusually large number for a butcher," Avatar said to Nigel.

Platt heaved a non-committal shrug. "I know of families naturally that large."

Avatar asked Chad, "What do you know of Ike?"

Chad momentarily considered the question. "Nice enough, in a gruff ill-tempered way. I've not heard of any unsavory encounters or trouble concerning him."

"You won't," said Platt in dispute. When Avatar appeared unconvinced, he admitted, "True, Ike can be gruff at times, but diligent and capable."

"Knowing his rough character, you considered him suitable for adopting so many orphans in such a short time?" challenged Avatar.

"Gruffness doesn't necessarily make him a bad father."

"Doesn't make him a good one either."

Platt abruptly turned from Avatar to Nigel. "Highness, you see by my records I take great care in placing the orphans in suitable homes."

"Personalities should also be a consideration."

Platt grew frustrated at Avatar's persistent argument. He continued his justification aimed at Nigel. "I give you my word, I will find an acceptable home for Alyson and Wyatt."

Nigel noticed Avatar's wariness, thus said to Platt, "Wyatt must have a kind, gentle, loving home that wouldn't drive him further into silence. Alyson also needs that, along with the capability to mold her strong will with proper guidance."

Platt frowned. "That might be hard to find in one home—"

"They will not be separated!" Nigel declared, as he rose to his feet.

The vehement reaction startled Platt. "Of course not, Highness. I was merely thinking out loud."

Nigel took a deep breath to regain his temper. "Although your records are well kept, I will visit Ike and Moreland."

"I shall inform my wife and accompany you." Platt turned for the door.

Avatar shook his head thus Nigel spoke in a nonchalant manner. "That won't be necessary. Sir Chad will serve as guide."

"But—," Platt's objection became stifled by a raised hand from Nigel. "Very well, Highness. I shall begin the search for a suitable family."

Upon return to their horses, Chad spoke. "Ike will be easy since his shop is off Market Square. Moreland's farm is more than an hour's ride from Hagley. It wouldn't do to miss our luncheon date since cats are notoriously agitated when hungry." He flashed a smile.

Nigel laughed. "Heaven forbid, I give her the opportunity to sharpen her claws."

"Just your presence does that," quipped Avatar.

"Then I'll find a way to declaw her before she can strike."

"You mean a bribe to save your hide," teased Chad.

"I learned that from Mirit," said Nigel with a gregarious smile. "We'll save the visit to Moreland's farm for another day."

It was the height of morning business when they arrived at Ike's butcher shop. Outside, Archie tended to chores. He hurried to greet them.

"Highness!"

"Good morning, Archie."

"When will you …" He stopped when Nigel clapped his shoulder.

"Signed and sealed this morning." Nigel held up his hand to show his signet ring.

Archie beamed. "Thank you!" He began to remove his soiled apron when "Archie!" boomed a voice from a large open window.

Ike's head and shoulder popped through. His physical appearance fit his voice. "Stop lollygagging and get back to work!"

"Master Ike, this is his Highness, Prince Nigel."

Ike's posture immediately changed to agreeable. "Oh, Your Highness. I almost didn't recognize you without your uniform."

Nigel huffed a wry snort. "I seem to get that a lot."

"Not that you are unrecognizable, no. Who wouldn't want to be visited by the queen's brother? Such a strong family resemblance."

Chad tried not to laugh at Ike's overly exaggerated attempt to curry favor. Avatar tossed a skeptical glance to Nigel. Neither were convinced by the effort.

"Actually, I came to tell Archie his adoption by Captain Dunsmore is finalized."

Ike's face fell. Upon catching the steady silver glare from Avatar, he hurried from the shop. He wiped bloody hands on his already soiled apron. "How wonderful for Archie." He patted the boy's shoulder and forced a smile.

"Will the captain, I mean, Papa come by to fetch me?" Archie eagerly asked Chad.

"He's at the manor waiting for you."

Nigel grinned. "He knew what I planned for this morning."

Again, Archie started to remove his apron, but sent a sheepish glance to Ike. "He said I didn't have to work here, if I didn't want. I could study to become a soldier like him."

"Far be it from me to counter your new father," Ike said with a begrudging stiffness.

Nigel frowned at Ike yet spoke to Archie. "Run along. We'll see you later."

Archie removed the apron, tossed it aside, and ran off.

"If you'll excuse me, Highness. Sir Chad. I have work." Ike started to depart when Nigel's question stopped him.

"Why did you want to adopt Archie?"

Ike heaved an awkward shrug. "I need help."

"From an orphan when you have three children of your own?"

Ike grew defensive. "My humble business can barely support the family I have. That's why Derek moved away when he wed, to relieve the burden. My youngest daughter is to wed next month, and with little dowry. A strong helper is necessary to survive."

"That still leaves a third child."

Ike expression fell with lament. "Ay, Maven. She will never wed. Her mind is not right. She needs constant care from my wife."

"What about the other six boys you adopted?" asked Avatar.

Ike blinked, puzzled. "I haven't adopted any boys. Archie was to be the first."

"Not according to Master Platt's ledger."

Stunned, Ike shook his head. "That can't be."

"Do not play games, Ike," began Chad firmly. "Platt's ledger states you adopted six boys over the last four years."

"My lord, there is a misunderstanding," began Ike with contrition. "I helped Master Platt to facilitate adoptions, not singularly adopt six boys."

"We found nothing in the ledger about aiding," said Avatar.

Ike became fretful. "I'm sure if you ask Platt, he will confirm what I tell you is true."

Loud complaining came from the shop. A distressed wife appeared in the backdoor threshold. "Ike!"

"Please, Highness, my customers."

Nigel nodded, so Ike hurried inside to his anxious wife. He and Chad and mounted the horses to leave. They said nothing until a few streets from the shop.

"Did you sense any falsehood?" Nigel asked Avatar.

"No, though it was hard to tell. He wouldn't look at me directly, while his body posture and voice often conflicted."

"Why would Platt record Ike as adopting all those boys?" asked Chad.

"Perhaps some of them were questionable," said Avatar.

Chad shook his head, unconvinced. "Platt is a good man. I can hardly imagine him doing anything questionable."

"I didn't say Platt, I said the adoptions."

"But he keeps the ledgers."

"Not all were written in the same hand."

Chad's head snapped around to look quizzically at Avatar. "You mean someone else recorded those adoptions, and Platt takes them at face value?"

"That's possible. Either way, it bears further investigation."

"After luncheon," said Nigel emphatically.

"You're going empty-handed?" bantered Avatar.

"No."

Chapter 8

NIGEL, CHAD, AND AVATAR REACHED THE APPOINTED INN FOR the luncheon rendezvous. Mirit, Magan, Virgil, Eli, Wyatt and Alyson sat at a large table with three vacant seats.

"I was beginning to wonder," Mirit said with thinly disguised annoyance. "We ordered luncheon. You'll have to accept what comes"

Nigel sat beside Alyson. "The shopkeeper delayed me longer than I would have liked." He noticed Alyson's hair freshly styled. She still wore her old, yet cleaned, clothes. Wyatt proudly beamed about his new suit. "Well, one of you is taken care of as far as clothes," he said with approval. "Your hair is very attractive," he complimented Alyson.

"Thank you," she demurely replied.

"The tailor is altering her dress. It will be ready after luncheon." Magan smiled and winked at Alyson, who giggled.

"The others will be sent to the manor when ready," added Mirit.

"Others?" asked Nigel before taking a drink from the tankard set before him by the innkeeper. The man also served Avatar and Chad.

"You didn't except us to only buy one dress and one suit, did you?" inquired Mirit.

Nigel simply shook his head and took a drink.

"So, it is true! You didn't want to see us get fitted or my hair done," chided Alyson.

"What?" exclaimed Nigel in surprise. He sent a questioning look to Mirit, who in turn spoke to Alyson.

"I said Nigel would join us after a special trip. Who told you otherwise?"

"The hairdresser says men always avoid their women when they get fitted or their hair done," insisted Alyson.

Nigel touched Alyson's arm to get her attention. Despite her avoiding eye contact, he noticed a hurt expression. "The hairdresser is wrong. I went to get something special to compliment your new dress."

She skeptically frowned. "What?"

"I meant to save it to complete your outfit, but since my veracity is called into question by a hairdresser." Nigel reached into his pocket to pull out a small, decorated box.

"A box?" said Alyson sarcastically.

"What's inside the box." He opened it for her to see.

She gasped with astonishment at seeing a gold necklace with a diamond pendant flanked by two amethyst stones.

Nigel smiled with pleasure at Alyson's reaction. "From what you told us, I reckoned your birthday in late summer, which is an amethyst birthstone. One for each you." He motioned between she and Wyatt. "Diamonds are the most precious gem." He placed it around her neck.

Momentarily speechless, Alyson stared at it. Her voice choked, and eyes misty. "No one's ever given me a gift." She flung her arms around Nigel's neck, and softly sobbed.

For a moment, Nigel held Alyson. He noticed Wyatt's sympathetic regard. "I didn't forget your brother."

Alyson sat up to wipe her eyes. "You didn't?"

Nigel reached into his other pocket. "I got a ring identical to your necklace." He gave the box to Wyatt. "Place it on the ring finger of the right hand. If it doesn't fit, we'll go back to have it sized."

Wyatt did so. He admired the slightly too large ring. He tried to speak the words, "Thank you," but mumbled.

"You're welcome."

Wyatt showed it to Mirit. She wore a deeply moved expression.

Nigel watched with satisfaction. This went better than he anticipated. The food arrived.

Wyatt became upset when the ring fell off his finger and onto the table when he started to eat. He looked with anxious fear at Nigel.

"We'll have it sized after luncheon, so it won't come off again," Nigel spoke with reassurance.

"I can take care of it now." Virgil placed the ring on Wyatt's right hand. He grasped the ring with his thumb and index finger while speaking, "*Na fainnean chun et na corragan,*" He pressed the metal to fit the boy's finger.

Wyatt flinched at feeling some pressure yet watched in fascination as the ring sunk to fit his finger.

"Now see if it will fall off," said Virgil. He made a motion with his hand for Wyatt to attempt to shake the ring loose. The boy mimicked the action. Much to his delight, the ring remained on his finger.

"Can he take it off at all?" asked Alyson.

Wyatt tugged. With a slight twist, the ring slipped off his finger. He widely smiled before he slipped it back on. He again tried to dislodge it by shaking his hand.

"I think that answers your question, mistress," said Virgil.

"I'm not a mistress. Why do you keep calling me that?"

"Remember what I told you," began Eli. "Guardians were created servants of Jor'el to protect Allon and mortals."

"So, they answer to us like we would a master?" she asked, a bit confused.

"Not exactly," said Nigel. "*Mistress* is a term of respect. The relationship between mortals and Guardians is mutually beneficial since we are all servants of Jor'el, who created everything."

"I'm not sure I understand," she said.

Wyatt regarded Virgil with thoughtful comprehension.

"I think your brother does," said Virgil.

Wyatt nodded. He turned to Alyson and made a gesture of linking hands. He pointed to Avatar, Virgil, and Skylar then linked his hands again.

"Ay, friends," said Skylar.

Wyatt vigorously nodded.

"We've never had friends," Alyson said soberly.

"You do now." Virgil smiled and added, "mistress."

She giggled. Wyatt went further in his discourse. He pointed to his ring then to her necklace. He indicated Nigel and Mirit then linked his hands again.

74

"Ay, we are your friends too," said Mirit. "And friends help each other without wanting or expecting anything in return."

Perplexed, Alyson regarded the pendant. "There's nothing we can help you with."

"Maybe not now. In the future, who knows?" said Nigel.

"That's right," began Chad. "I too wondered about that when I became Nigel's squire. Over the course of many years, our friendship has grown to where we help each other."

"You have to start somewhere." Eli touched the necklace. He sat on the other side of Alyson.

The innkeeper arrived with a young man in tow. He bowed to Mirit. "Compliments of my master, Princess. The dress is ready. It can be fitted to the young lady at your convenience."

"We'll be there once we have finished dining."

"Is the food satisfactory, Princess?" the innkeeper asked.

"Indeed, Master Sutcliff."

Sutcliff grinned at the twins. "I have an extra special treat the children might enjoy. Chocolate cake. The grocer had a special delivery of cocoa."

Wyatt looked confused and shrugged.

"Have you never eaten chocolate before?" Eli asked.

Wyatt shook his head. Alyson also answered negatively.

"It's one of my favorite desserts. Cook always makes it for my birthday." Eli then spoke to the innkeeper. "Two large pieces, Master Sutcliff."

A few moments later, Sutcliff returned with the specified dessert. He placed one before each of the children.

Alyson quizzically regarded the cake. "Looks like a very dark gingerbread."

"Oh, it's better than gingerbread," said Eli merrily.

Wyatt took a sniff. He used his fork to take a bit. His eyes danced with delight. He eagerly ate the cake.

"Easy, not so fast," chuckled Mirit.

Alyson took a bite. "Oh, this is good!"

Nigel used his fork to steal a piece of Alyson's cake.

"I thought knights don't steal."

"We don't. We share."

She pushed the plate toward him.

"Enjoy. I was only teasing," chuckled Nigel.

She jerked the plate back with a triumphant grin. "So was I."

Chapter 9

COLBY AND VANCE MANAGED TO ENTER HAGLEY WITHOUT attracting attention. Then again, their faces were not as familiar or loathed as Darnel. Still, they maintained a humble posture to mingle with the crowd and avoid any soldiers.

At one point, they hid in an alley when soldiers rode past. This happened to be across from the inn where the royal party dined. Colby seized Vance when the group emerged.

"Darnel was right. They did come this way," said Colby.

"I recognize Sir Chad and his wife. Not the others," said Vance.

"I think the one on the left is the prince Dunsmore mentioned."

"That would make sense with Guardians in attendance."

They watched the group walk a few blocks from the inn to the dress maker's shop.

"What do we do? We can't get at them," chided Colby.

"Tell father. But first, let's find out what our friend knows." Vance led Colby from the alley.

❧

Nigel fidgeted, as they waited for the dressmaker to finish fitting Alyson. Avatar, Skylar, and Virgil stood just inside the door near the large shop window. Mirit, Magan, Eli, and Chad sat patiently in the four shop chairs. Wyatt dozed on Eli's lap. He became sleepy after lunch. Mirit smirked at Eli, and indicated Nigel, who paced by the window.

Chad approached Nigel. "I don't think I've seen this side of you. Antsy at a simple fitting."

Nigel cocked a wry grin. "You didn't see how nervous I was trying to decide what suit to wear for my wedding. Poor Harold. I kept wishing you were there to help."

"Really? You never told me that."

"Thinking back on it, even your presence wouldn't have helped. Isn't that right, Avatar?"

Avatar stared intently out the window.

"Avatar? Did you hear me?" Nigel repeated, curious at the Guardian's distraction. Met again with silence, he moved to see what captured such attention.

Avatar briefly glanced at Nigel then pointed to the object of interest. Burt stood across the street in a manner suggesting observance of the shop. Ike arrived. He spoke what appeared to be angry words to Burt. When Ike caught sight of them watching, the two men hurried off in opposite directions.

"Oh! It fits wonderfully," they heard Mirit exclaim. "Nigel, don't you agree?"

While Nigel was forced to shift his focus to join Mirit, Avatar noticed a dark, cloaked and hooded figure in an opposite doorway shadow. The figure nodded at him then disappeared. No light just vanished.

Impressed, Nigel smiled at seeing Alyson wore a dress of rich dark green with light green brocade and gold trim. "Indeed. The cut, style, and color are wonderful compliments to your flaxen hair and petty hazel eyes." He winked at her. She deeply blushed with uncertainty.

Mirit inspected the dress. "Nicely done, Master Tailor." She turned Alyson to the full-length mirror.

A low gasp escaped when Alyson saw herself. "I never thought to have such a fine dress." She felt the necklace. She fought back tears, as she gazed at her reflection. In the mirror, she noticed Nigel stand beside her.

"A beautiful young lady a prince knight would willingly escort anywhere." He offered his arm. She accepted, and they departed the store.

Mirit motioned to Virgil. The Guardian paid the tailor while the others left the shop.

When Virgil rejoined them, mortals had mounted horses and entered the carriage for the return trip. He stiffened and gripped his sword. His eyes darted back and forth, as if searching for a presence.

"Did you sense it too?" Skylar whispered.

"Ay. Again, too quick for identification."

Skylar noticed Avatar shut the carriage door. "Avatar instructed Mona and her Trio Mates to investigate the sense from earlier. Maybe it was one of them and not anything threatening."

"Perhaps," said Virgil, not fully convinced. "We'll stay close and ready."

The conversation stopped when Avatar approached. "Escort them back to the manor."

"Ay, Commander," Virgil acknowledged.

Avatar stepped back into the shadows to avoid being seen by the departing mortals. Once everyone was out of sight, he proceeded to the orphanage. He made his way to the rear where he discovered the back gate locked.

"*Fosgail,*" he whispered. Click! The gate opened. "Move sight unseen by mortal eyes," he spoke in the Ancient before he entered the compound.

While the day's activity buzzed all around, Avatar walked in the midst of them to the kitchen. He didn't see Burt. Perhaps he arrived before the mortal could return. The kitchen staff didn't notice him, as he wandered about the room. He paused before a desk littered with papers. He picked up a piece to examine the handwriting. He tucked it in his belt and left.

From the kitchen, Avatar proceeded to Platt's office. With the door already opened, he walked in. No one. At the shelf containing the adoption ledgers, he pulled out a specific book. He flipped a few pages. Finding what he wanted, he compared the writing between the ledger and paper from the kitchen. He slammed the book closed and replaced it. Hearing mortal footsteps, and recognizing Platt's voice, Avatar quietly said, "Appear as normal for mortal sight."

Startled, Platt stopped in the threshold. "Commander?" Confused, he glanced outside then back to Avatar. "I didn't notice your arrival."

"Master Platt," Avatar casually said, not commenting on the mortal's surprise.

Recovered from the momentary bewilderment, Platt asked, "Is there something I can help you with? Or did the Prince send you to make inquiry about my progress?"

Avatar held out the paper. "Whose handwriting is this?"

Platt took it for examination. "Burt. It's a grocery list," he replied nonchalant.

"How does Burt know Ike?"

Platt shrugged, ignorance. "I don't know. Friends, family. I really couldn't begin to guess."

"Does Burt help you record adoptions?"

"No. I do them myself."

Avatar's silver eyes stared at Platt, which made the mortal uncomfortable. "I will ask you again. Does Burt help you record adoptions?"

"No. I do them myself."

In a quick, almost imperceptible move, Avatar fetched the ledger and opened to the page. "How do you explain that all records of Ike and Moreland's adoptions are done in Burt's handwriting?" He snatched the paper from Platt to place it, and the ledger, on the desk.

Momentarily unable to reply, Platt stared at them. "It looks more like mine than Burt's."

"Or a bad forgery. The truth!" demanded Avatar.

"Upon my word, Commander, I do them. This is an older ledger." He hastily crossed to the shelves. "These are all older. The current ledger is in my desk under lock and key." He returned to the desk, where he attempted to open the middle draw to show it locked. "The key is always in my possession." He pulled it out from being tucked inside his belt and attached to the belt by a chain.

Again, Avatar's silver gaze intensified. The mortal trembled but withstood the scrutiny. "Something is questionable about those adoptions. With or without your cooperation, I will discover the truth."

Avatar left the orphanage, in full view of anyone who bothered to notice.

Chapter 10

ESPITE THE ACTIVITY OF THE DAY, ALYSON COULDN'T SLEEP. Although tired, her mind filled with images and questions. All the new experiences felt overwhelming, and a bit confusing. From a hungry runaway one day, to be treated like a princess the next. She moved her head enough to see Virgil and Skylar remained. Eli retired after seeing them to bed.

Guardians were almost magical in a scary, yet comforting way. Remembering what Virgil did to fit Wyatt's ring made Alyson touch the necklace she still wore. Night made it difficult to see the true beauty of the necklace. Tears welled up, and she wiped her eyes. *Why?* was the question that dominated her mind.

She quietly rolled over and nudged her brother. "Wyatt," she whispered. He didn't move. "Wyatt," she said a little louder. She added a rough shake on his shoulder. At his groan, she again looked to the Guardians. They didn't react.

She inched closer his face. "Wyatt, wake-up."

His eyes opened. He gave a brief start at seeing her right in his face.

"*Shhh,*" she warned. A third glance at the Guardians. Nothing. They simply stood in their places.

"Al ... lee?" he stuttered in a quiet question.

"Do you like them?"

Wyatt stirred to raise up and turn his head.

"No, I mean *them*. The princess and prince knight."

He smiled and nodded.

"Why?" she whispered.

He brought out his hand to show the ring.

She touched the necklace. "Ay, they bought us these, and clothes. But *why?*" she stressed.

"H … e … lp." He brought his hands together.

"Adults don't help without wanting something," she said in weak refute.

Wyatt pointed to the Guardians.

"They said they were created to help."

Again, he brought his hands together.

"We've never had friends before," she lamented.

He held up his ring, pointed to it, and the Guardians. He then made the sign for sleep.

"You can sleep because we have friends now."

He nodded. He tapped the necklace then gently pushed Alyson's head to the pillow. He made the sign for sleep.

"I'll try."

He reached for her hand. Holding her hand, he fell back asleep. Soon, Alyson too slept.

***

The following morning was the weekly day set aside to honor the Almighty. Mirit and Nigel didn't engage in weapons practice. Instead they took the time to refresh and relax before breakfast. This morning Mirit worn a day gown. With Virgil looking after the children, she again fixed her own hair. In the cooler weather, she wore it partially down. She glanced in the mirror to Nigel, who sat to pull on his boots.

"You haven't told me anything about the visit to Platt," she said.

"Everything went well." He put on the second boot then crossed to the vanity. "I made certain he understood they are to be kept together. *And* the family *must* meet with our approval."

She shied from him to complete her hair by brushing the loose locks into place.

"Mirit, it is for the best to find them a family."

She put the brush down to look at him by way of the mirror. "Alyson wouldn't take off the necklace even when I said she shouldn't sleep with it on."

His expression told her the news struck him. Her touch on his arm prompted an attempt at levity. "I may not enjoy shopping *with* women, but I do know how to shop *for* them."

A tender smile appeared. "You've always had a soft side for the women in your life."

"Well, this is only temporary."

Her smile faded when she stood to confront him. "Temporary or not, they need our undivided attention. So, promise me, no further trips to the orphanage to discuss the matter with Platt. Let him do his work and contact us. Above all, don't mention him to Alyson." When he hesitated with indecision, she added, "You told him the family must meet with our approval. In truth, there is nothing more you can do until then. However, you *can* help Alyson and Wyatt prepare for the new family."

He nodded in agreement. "Very well."

"You promise? As a prince knight?" She fought a smile.

"I promise. As a prince knight. I will not contact Platt and give them my undivided attention."

⁂

After breakfast, everyone attended the weekly service held in the manor chapel. Located on the east wall of the compound, the chapel was a modest-sized building with enough seating to accommodate two dozen people. The twins sat between Nigel and Mirit. Magan and Chad sat side-by-side with Chandler beside Magan, and Ephrim on the other side of Chad. Such competitive sons where best kept apart during service for ease of control and discipline. The boys' nurses, Dunsmore, and Archie sat, while Ambrose and servants respectfully stood. The Guardians also attended.

Occasionally, Wyatt glanced at the book Nigel held open on his lap. Nigel appeared to read along with the priest. Although they didn't know the words to any songs, Alyson and Wyatt listened and watched the others participate.

At one point, Nigel noticed Wyatt's interest, so he gently moved the book toward the boy to share. The gesture made Wyatt slump back and bite his lip.

Nigel leaned down to whisper. "It's all right. You can read along also."

Wyatt scooted closer to Alyson, flushed with embarrassment. With confused curiosity, Nigel glanced to Mirit, who made a careful shrug of ignorance. With discretion, Alyson touched the book, pointed to her eye then Wyatt's head. Nigel's expression showed he understood. He assumed a neutral posture, as he returned his attention to the sermon. After a couple of moments, Wyatt again made a circumspect attempt to view the pages. Nigel pretended not to notice.

When leaving the chapel, Nigel handed the book to Wyatt, so he could speak with the priest. Wyatt took it, though appeared uncertain. After a brief conversation, Nigel held Wyatt's shoulder to guide him from the building. He leaned down to speak in a casual, private tone.

"There is no shame in admitting a weakness. Quite the contrary. By admitting them, we can grow. I had to admit that when I was younger.

"U …? P-p-pri … nce?" Wyatt stumbled over the words.

"Ay. Me. A prince. Despite the title, I'm just a person with strengths and weaknesses like everyone else." He motioned to the book.

Wyatt's brows furrowed in deep consideration, as he stared at the book. His struggle to communicate visible. He held up the book then used it to make a swinging motion. "Le … nnn." Frustrated at being unable to get the word out clearly, he made the motion again: the book and a swing.

"I believe he wants to learn to read just like how to handle a sword," Virgil surmised.

Despite a flush of embarrassment, Wyatt pointed up at Virgil, and nodded.

Hearing the exchange, Alyson spoke in distressed refute. "He doesn't remember much."

Wyatt huffed in annoyance at her. He held up the book in defiance. He slapped the cover in frustration, motioned to his head, and sneered.

"Easy," Mirit tried to calm Wyatt. "Alyson is merely concerned for you."

"St-st … p." He stuck his chest. "Me—"

"You think she's stopping you?"

Wyatt adamantly shook his head.

"I believe he doesn't want his lack of memory to stop him," Virgil suggested.

Again, Wyatt motioned affirmatively at Virgil.

Nigel widely smiled. "Since that is your desire, I believe now is a good time for your first lesson in reading."

"Now? Luncheon will be ready shortly," said Mirit.

"It's good to reinforce the experience with further training." Nigel patted Wyatt's shoulder. "Don't you agree?"

Wyatt made an attempt at saying, "Ay."

"You take Mistress Aly—cat for her first etiquette lesson before luncheon while I see to Master Wyatt's education."

Wyatt smirked and waved a finger at Alyson

"You think he's funny!" Alyson stuck out her tongue.

"I'm told humor is one of my best qualities when dealing with females." Nigel winked at Wyatt.

Alyson placed hands on her hips and stomped her foot.

"Come. Let me explain how to deal with male humor." Mirit took Alyson's hand to move away. "Don't be too long," she said over her shoulder to Nigel.

Nigel took Wyatt to the manor library. The boy's eyes widened at the number of books. He tugged on Nigel's sleeve. He moved in a circle, as he pointed to the shelves.

Nigel chuckled. "Actually, this is small compared to the library at Waldron."

"Wa …?" he shrugged.

"Waldron has been the King's castle for many centuries. It's where I grew up, and live part of the year as The King's Champion. The rest of the time I'm at the Fortress of Jor'el in the Region of Sanctuary since I'm also First Jor'ellian."

Wyatt's considering glance passed from Nigel to the shelves.

"The book of Verse maybe a bit difficult." Nigel took the book from Wyatt to place on a table. "I think the best one to start with is Prophecy. It also includes history."

Nigel crossed to a stand upon which sat an open book. He removed it to place on the same table as with his book. He scooted over a second chair for Wyatt to sit. Once both were comfortable, Nigel flipped a few pages.

Using a finger to follow the words, Nigel read the sentence out loud *"Only the most dedicated Jor'ellian can become a knight of Allon."*

Wyatt's brows deeply furrowed with concentration as he listened and followed Nigel's finger. He tapped on the page.

"Jor'ellian," Nigel repeated the word. When Wyatt appeared confused, Nigel said, "We sound out words. Like this. *Jor—ral—lee—an.* Jor'ellian. Ignore the accent mark between the *r* and *e*."

Wyatt frowned and sheepishly glanced aside.

"When you know what letters sound like, you can do it in your mind, not just speaking." Nigel considered the boy for a moment. "I might have to use a primer to teach you the alphabet first."

Wyatt shook his head in frowning dispute. He used his finger to circle a letter within the sentence. "A…a".

Impressed, Nigel said, "You recognize letters. That's good. Who taught you?"

Wyatt flushed with embarrassment when he indicated his head.

"I doubt the person you ran from provided such instruction."

Wyatt slowly shook his head.

"My guess would be your grandmother. I learned the alphabet when I was five and could read by myself when I was six."

Wyatt nodded. Again, he touched his head.

"You said you didn't want your lack of memory to stop you. In reality, speaking a little, and recognizing letters, shows your memory is healing. I know what it's like to recover from great injury."

"U ...?"

"The injury I suffered nearly killed me. I couldn't walk or talk. My face, and the entire left side of my body was broken."

Wyatt quizzically examined Nigel, which caused Nigel to grin.

"Jor'el healed me."

Wyatt folded his hands together in a prayerful posture and looked up at the ceiling.

"Ay, the Almighty. From what I see, Jor'el is doing the same with you."

Wyatt concentrated on the page again. He placed his finger on the word *Jor'ellian*. He struggled to form the word.

"Let's start with something easy. Here." Nigel pointed to a different word. "Knight. That's me also."

"U ...?" Wyatt indicated both words *Jor'ellian* and *knight*. He then puffed out his chest and flexed his arms like muscles.

"I am strong due to training."

Wyatt shook his head and made the gestures again.

Nigel tried to guess. "Important?"

Wyatt vigorously nodded.

"Well, I suppose, since I'm the next in authority after the King and Vicar. Of course, the Almighty is supreme over everything."

Wyatt stared at the word *knight*. His finger tracing under the word several times.

"I assume you're trying to sound it out in your mind."

Wyatt scrunched his face and tapped the letter.

"K. Sounds like *ka*."

Wyatt titled his head quizzically in regard of the word. "*Ka ... ni ...*"

Nigel grinned at the attempt. "No, in this case the *k* is silent. *Knight* sounds just like *night* as is darkness."

Wyatt screwed up his face in disagreeing skepticism.

Nigel fought a laugh at the expression. "Don't look at me that way. I didn't write the grammar rules."

Wyatt frowned. This time, he slumped back in the chair.

"Reading isn't too difficult."

Wyatt patted his stomach.

Nigel smiled with understanding. "Very well. Food before more study."

While taking Wyatt to the private dining room, Nigel thought about what just happened. He hadn't realized the similarities with Wyatt until speaking about his past accident. *Broken.* The word kept echoing in his mind. Both suffered at the hands of malevolent individuals; his by a rogue Guardian, and Wyatt's by a heartless man. Morrell eventually paid for his crimes, but Wyatt's assailant remains at large.

For the boy's sake, Nigel suppressed his rising anger at anyone who abuses a child. Still, the commonality of affliction touched him, yet so did the differences. He was sixteen, while Wyatt only ten. Perhaps his tender age helped to offset full recollection of the traumatic event. Despite the severity and lack of memory, it didn't appear to affect Wyatt's trusting nature. Nigel fought cynicism during his years of wandering. That was more like Alyson. No, Wyatt showed amazing trust and willingness to learn, something Nigel felt needed to be encouraged. Perhaps with it, the boy could heal.

In the private dining room, the others assembled. Eli stood on the far side of the room speaking to Alyson. Wyatt joined them. Nigel went to the sideboard to fetch a cup of hard cider. A sentimental smile grew, as he watched the twins interact with his nephew. Ever since early childhood, Eli exhibited enormous patience and empathy toward others.

Avatar approached. For moment Nigel appeared not to notice, so Avatar followed his gaze. "A familiar scene."

"How so?" Nigel took a drink.

"Eli shows the patience you once did with Tristine and Necie. You tolerated much from them."

"My thoughts were about Wyatt. I hadn't realized until after chapel the similarities we share. Oh, true different circumstances and manifestations, but both broken and struggling to be whole again." Nigel took a drink to swallow back the lump in his throat.

"There are also similarities in nature. As soon as you could hold a sword, you begged me to teach you Guardian techniques. He shows an enthusiasm to learn. Eager to defend and protect. He soothes Alyson like you did Tristine."

"She has sharper claws than Tristine," Nigel muttered, more into his cup. His regard of the twins turned thoughtful. "I fear what will happen if we get too close. When Platt finds a family, Mirit may be devastated."

Avatar gripped Nigel's arm. "Don't let fear guide you. Remember what happened last time."

Nigel slightly quivered. Indeed. Last time, fear kept him from speaking truthfully to his father on that fateful hunting trip. The one in which his family believed him killed.

Avatar's hand moved from Nigel's arm to his shoulder. "Don't neglect your own heart. It's too important to ignore." He made a nod in the direction of the table where the others gathered.

A bit disconcerted, Nigel took a drink to recover.

"Luncheon!" Magan announced.

Chapter 11

URING THE NEXT TEN DAYS, MAKING WYATT AND ALYSON FEEL safe and comfortable took priority. Nigel kept his word to Mirit and neither spoke of Platt nor sent inquiry. Although he knew Avatar meant him when speaking of fear, Nigel used it as motivation to aid the twins. Allaying their fears became his focus, especially Alyson. Despite spending more time with Wyatt for training and studies, he made certain to give Alyson his undivided attention when together. She seemed to respond, though with the occasional verbal jab. Nigel soon became grateful that Platt sent no word regarding a new family. Growing attachment became hard to ignore, nor did he want to set it aside.

In the mornings, Wyatt joined him, Avatar, and Eli for training and practice. He made certain Wyatt used a wooden sword for instruction. During the first week, Nigel observed Wyatt's bouts with Eli, to get a sense of the boy's form. The past few days, he personally engaged Wyatt. Each day saw a marked improvement in Wyatt's attitude and skill. He still stuttered when trying to speak, but words came more frequently. Eagerness marked his character.

Pleased, Nigel disengaged from a bout. "Excellent Wyatt! I'm impressed by how remarkably well you've done in so short a time."

"I … like lear … ning."

"And it shows. Perhaps, we can try something else." Nigel used the towel Eli gave him to wipe his face.

"Real …" Wyatt pointing to the wooden sword he held.

"Tomorrow. And we shall incorporate Jor'ellian principles, those I use to instruct cadets. I'm now confident, you can handle it."

"Prin … see … puls?"

Nigel grinned. "Principles." When Wyatt still appeared perplexed, he explained. "Principles are fundament truths that guide us."

"Ver … se … Prop … a see?"

"Ay. Those principles form the basis tenets for training a Jor'ellian knight. They help us defend Jor'el and those we love."

Wyatt appeared perplexed. "How …?"

"How does it help?" Nigel asked and received a nod from Wyatt. "A Jor'ellian knight diligently applies justice, peace, and righteousness to daily life. By incorporating Verse and Prophecy, we learn from our mistakes, and grow. Armed with all that, we defend Jor'el, safeguard the kingdom, and protect those dear to us."

Wyatt pointed to Avatar and Skylar. "They teach you … of Jor'el like …?" He held up the wooden sword before placing it away for the day.

Nigel nodded. "Ay, such as you and I have been doing with reading lessons. Only now, we shall apply those principles to defense. Make them go from the page to reality."

"Skylar has helped me live what I've learned, especially when younger. He can help you too," Eli offered.

Wyatt gazed up at Skylar with uncertainty.

Nigel patted Wyatt's shoulder. "Avatar was my Overseer during childhood." He laughed in remembrance. "I can't begin to tell you how many times I needed his help to apply what I *thought* I learned."

Wyatt glanced with determination at Skylar and Avatar. "Learn … apply, and … this," he pointed to the sword. "Make me," he thumped his chest, and tugged at the ring he wore, "be like … prince."

Moved by Wyatt's desire, Nigel glanced to Avatar. For a brief moment, he held the Guardian's encouraging gaze before Avatar warmly smiled at Wyatt. "I believe we can make that happen."

"Indeed," Nigel agreed.

"How? If find other … fam …"

Nigel drew Wyatt to sit on a bench. He lifted the hand upon which Wyatt wore the ring. He placed his hand next to Wyatt to show his signet ring. "You already found one."

"U? P-p-pr … ince!" Excited, Wyatt sat up straight and tall.

"Me. Only *father*, not prince."

Wyatt tightly embraced Nigel. "Make fa-th-er proud."

"I know you will." Feeling a bit overwhelmed, Nigel nudged Wyatt. "Now, run along with Eli and clean up for breakfast." He fought back a sniffle to watch the departure.

Nigel felt Avatar's hand on his shoulder. "I'm glad you took my advice."

"Things always turned out better when I did." Nigel tenderly smiled. "Mirit said she wasn't looking to arbitrarily fill the void. Somehow, this isn't arbitrary, and discovered a void I didn't think existed." He took a deep settling breath and stood. "Inform Platt to fill out all the necessary papers."

With great pleasure, Avatar said, "Consider it done."

<hr />

While Wyatt joined the men in daily training, Mirit and Magan paid special attention to Alyson. Mirit personally saw to Alyson's morning toiletry, since the girl was unaccustomed to servants.

"Your hair is looking much better after diligent pampering." Mirit styled Alyson's hair. The girl sat in front of the vanity mirror. "What do you think?"

Alyson turned her head to various angles to observe the style. "In some ways, I like it, but in others, I'm not sure."

"Why?"

Alyson's shrug and lowered eyes.

Mirit knelt beside the bench. "Tell me what is troubling you."

Alyson shrugged, again hesitant. "Everything is so different. I'm not sure how to feel. I mean …"

"What?" Mirit stroked Alyson's cheek.

"Why ask that man to find us a family?" Alyson bolted up. "Why do all this for us only to give us away!" She ran from the room weeping.

"Alyson!" Mirit dashed after the girl only to find the hallway empty. Virgil came down the corridor carrying a tray with a pitcher and basin. "Have you seen Alyson?" she hurriedly asked.

"No, why?"

"She became upset and ran out of the room. I didn't see which way she went."

Virgil set the tray on a hall table then closed his eyes. He opened his eyes and spoke with reassurance. "She's nearby. There is nothing to fear within these walls."

"Maybe not physically." She gripped his arm with urgency. "Find her quickly. I need to … just find her!"

Virgil moved toward the back stairs just as Nigel came from the opposite direction. Nigel smiled at Mirit.

"Well, is the cat more subdued this morning after—"

"Why must you humiliate her by calling her names? And why did you have to speak to Platt?" She ran back to the chamber and slammed the door.

Hearing a click, Nigel tried the door to find it locked. "Mirit?" He tried to curb his temper when he tried the knob again. "Mirit. Open the door," he firmly said.

Click.

Nigel entered, only more gently in shutting the door. Visibly emotional, Mirit moved away from him. "What upset you so much as to lock the door on me? You've never done that before."

"Alyson ran out, upset because *you* told Platt to find them a family!"

"It was natural to speak with him since they are orphans."

"But *why*? That is what she asked. Why take them in and do all we have to give them away …" Mirit sobbed so deeply she had to sit. "That is what she accused us of doing before she ran off."

Pricked, Nigel winced with remorse. "I'll find her."

"Virgil is doing that," Mirit managed to say before weeping some more.

He held her. "I'm sorry. At the time, I thought it was the right thing to do," he spoke soft apologetic words. He gently wiped the tears from her face. "The past ten days have brought a gladness to my heart, I never thought to feel. Or rather, didn't think I needed to feel."

Mirit sat up, hopeful. "What are you saying?"

"A few moments ago, Wyatt said he wanted to be like me, and tugged on the ring." Nigel did an emotional laugh. "Somehow those words filled me with a pride and joy I never experienced before. I convinced myself we didn't need children to be happy. That our nieces and nephews were enough."

Mirit gasped with delight. "You mean?"

"I sent Avatar to have Platt prepare the necessary papers for *us* to become parents."

Mirit hugged his neck, as she wept tears of joy.

"Now, I have to chase down a cat." He kissed her.

Nigel went in the same direction as Virgil. Find the Guardian, and he would find Alyson. The back stairs led to the servants' hall. Once there, he inquired of a maid if she had seen Virgil. She indicated the door leading to the back courtyard. A seven-and-half-foot Guardian warrior was not difficult to find. In fact, Virgil casually stood in front of a shed at the side of the stables.

Nigel fought a smile, as he approached. "I take it our cat is cornered," he whispered. Before he received an affirmative from Virgil, he heard soft sobs coming from the shed. His humor faded to pain at hearing the grief. He gripped Virgil's arm and drew the Guardian close to the door. "Mirit said she sent you to find Alyson to tell her the good news." Nigel spoke more to the door than Virgil. "Though you realize this means you will have to call her *princess* instead of *mistress*."

Virgil widely smiled with understanding. "Princess Alyson or Princess Ally Cat?"

Nigel laughed. "That depends if she thinks a prince knight will make a good father."

The shed door began to open. Alyson cautiously poked her head out. "I thought you told *that* man to find us a family?"

Nigel tenderly regarded her. "Spending time with you and Wyatt changed my mind and heart." He reached to touch her necklace. "This now belongs to *my* daughter."

The door swung open, and Alyson embraced Nigel.

"I guess the drowned rat doesn't look so bad now, eh *princess?*" Virgil quipped.

"Princess? I just got used to being called mistress."

Nigel chuckled. "Come. *Your* mother is worried."

When they arrived back at the apartment, Eli and Wyatt were there. Wyatt happily spoke with Mirit. Or least, used words along with excited gestures. Upon sight of Alyson, Wyatt ran to embrace his sister.

"Parents!" He motioned to Nigel and Mirit. He joined his hands together. "Family."

"That's right," agreed Mirit. "Did Nigel tell you?" she asked Alyson. The girl embraced Mirit. Hearing a soft sniffle, Mirit kissed Alyson's forehead. "No need to cry."

"I didn't think we would ever find a family again." Alyson buried her head against Mirit.

Mirit led Alyson to sit on the sofa. "You have. Now, you are safe, well-cared for, and most of all, loved."

"You are now my cousins," said Eli. He placed an arm around Wyatt's shoulder.

Alyson became a bit fretful. "Your father is the king!"

"And now your uncle, since my sister is queen," said Nigel, matter of fact.

"No need to be afraid," said Eli. "My father is a very kind man. He will gladly welcome you both."

"What do we call him?" Alyson tentatively asked Eli.

"Well, in private, uncle. In public, even I call him *Sire* or *Your Majesty,* as a show of respect."

Mirit took Alyson's hands to get her attention. "Overtime, you will learn all the necessary protocol for being a member of the royal family. For now, let us celebrate."

Alyson earnest regarded Mirit. "What do I call you? *Princess* when in public?"

Mirit lightly chuckled. "For now, *Marmi* would be nice. That's what I called my mother when I was little."

Alyson flashed a glance to Nigel then asked Mirit, "What did you call your father?"

"Papa."

Alyson sat up straight to face Nigel. She fought a smile. "Papa prince knight."

"Papa drowned rat," Mirit wryly said with a wink at Alyson.

"I think just *Papa* will serve," Nigel laughed.

"Papa!" Wyatt declared, and stood proudly beside Nigel.

Chapter 12

AVATAR SPENT THE REST OF THE MORNING HELPING PLATT with the necessary paperwork for adoption. After his discovery of doctored ledgers, he wanted to make certain everything was handled properly.

Several times Platt cast uncertain glances in his direction but uttered not a word of dispute or acted uncooperative. By what he could sense from the mortal, Platt felt uneasy and nervous, not deceptive. He chose not to press Platt about the different handwriting. Instead, Avatar paid careful attention to Platt's handling of the paperwork, ledger notations, and affixing of the official seal.

Leaving the orphanage, Avatar thought to take advantage of being away from the manor to continue his investigation. He passed the butcher shop where a quick observation told him nothing appeared out of the ordinary.

He circled back to a narrow street that intersected the alley behind the orphanage. This time he caught sight of Burt speaking with a younger man, perhaps twenty years of age. Cautious and careful, the young man handed Burt a pouch. Burt appeared to use his hand as if weighing the contents. Satisfied, Burt patted the young man's shoulder and returned inside the orphanage. The other hastened down the alley opposite Avatar.

Rather than accost Burt, Avatar found a deserted area near the city's western wall. He closed his eyes to stretch out his senses. A few moments later, Mona appeared.

"Report," he snapped.

"Darnel moves his camp from place to place around Hagley. Probably to avoid suspicion. Kendra has kept watch of Ike but had not found evidence to connect him to Burt."

"Moreland?"

Mona answered a bit hesitantly. "Dale is …"

"Uncooperative?"

"No. She is playing her part. Though not happy about it." At his frown, she said, "You know such deception goes against our nature. She may be combative, but she is dedicated."

Avatar's frown deepened. "Something is going on, and I'm certain it involves Burt. Just a few moments ago, I saw him with another individual exchanging what appeared to be a money pouch. Perhaps payment of some kind."

"You don't know the other's identity?"

Avatar shook his head. "I've not seen him before. A younger man with light brown hair, clean face. No more than twenty mortal years."

"He sounds like Colby. Darnel's youngest son."

Avatar's look turned sharp. "If he is paying Burt …"

"Then that could be our connection," she concluded.

"I believe it is time to *officially* involve the King's Champion."

The statement surprised Mona. "But the children …"

Avatar genuinely smiled. He pulled folded papers from his belt. "Done."

"Wonderful. Kendra and Dale will be glad to hear it."

Avatar tucked the papers back under his belt. He grew thoughtful. "After our visit to Moreland, have Dale provoke Darnel into action."

"Very well." Mona stepped back and vanished in dimension travel.

***

At the manor, Avatar arrived at a celebration held in the private courtyard. The pleasant late-autumn day offered a chance to enjoy the outdoors. Chandler and Ephrim raced about with Wyatt and Eli in pursuit. Virgil and Skylar herded Chandler and Eli to keep them within the courtyard. Magan held Niles on her lap while Alyson knelt and made the infant giggle. Mirit enjoyed watching Alyson interact with Niles. Chad and Nigel laughed at the boys.

For several delightful moments, Avatar watched the scene. With a large smile, he approached Nigel and Chad. He handed Nigel the papers. "It is now official."

Nigel gaped at sight of the Jor'ellian seal. "Who signed it?" he asked, accepting the papers.

"Me, of course. *Commander* of the Jor'ellian Guards. Next to you, the King, and Kell, I do have the authority to sign certain official documents." His hand on Nigel's shoulder brought the prince's attention from the papers. "It was my great privilege to do so. My only regret, is that in my position, I can't be their Overseer like I was yours."

Nigel's impish gaze shifted from Wyatt back to Avatar. "The *old Guardian* can still help with my son's training."

After a chuckle of agreement, Avatar's expression turned serious. "When you have a moment, we three need to speak. I discovered more inaccuracies." He nodded to Chad.

Understanding, Chad replied. "Not having a nap, the boys will soon be off to bed. We can talk then."

Shortly after sunset, Magan, Mirit, and Alyson left to put Niles, Chandler and Ephrim to bed. Virgil carried the tired twin boys. Nigel spoke a private word to Eli to occupy Wyatt so he and Chad could slip away with Avatar.

"By inaccuracies, I take it you mean Platt's ledgers," Nigel began.

"Ay. Apparently, all adoptions were not recorded in his handwriting. Specifically, those dealing with Ike and Moreland," said Avatar.

"Are you certain?" asked Chad, disturbed.

"I found a comparable hand that matched those entries. It appears to be Burt, the orphanage cook."

Stymied for a moment, Chad gaped at Avatar. "Why?"

"I'm not certain yet. However, I saw him earlier today with another man believed to be Darnel's son, Colby."

The news angered Chad. "Darnel is in Hagley!" He moved, "Duns—"

"Not Darnel." Avatar seized Chad whose temper was slow to cool.

Nigel added his voice to help Chad calm down. "Let Avatar finish! Then we'll decide how to proceed."

The Guardian's pointed gaze shifted between them. "There is more to my coming here than a simple holiday visit. In truth, I'm here on assignment from Kell and Tyrone."

"Why didn't you tell us before now?" asked Nigel.

Avatar tried to wave it aside. "There are multiple reasons, but the one needed for this conversation is to stop a gang of slave traders working in the province."

"I told you!" Chad chided to Nigel.

Nigel waved Chad silent to focus on Avatar. "You believe Platt is involved?"

"If he is, I'll make him pay!" Chad swore.

"Enough!" Nigel warned. "I understand this is extremely personal to you. It also is to me, and just not because of our relationship. Allow Avatar to proceed without interruption."

Chad tightly pressed his lips together to still his temper.

"I'm uncertain about Platt's involvement," began Avatar. "Each time I see him, I sense an uneasiness of cautious nervousness, not total deception. We know Darnel is a key figure, along with his family. Ike denies anything."

"We saw him with Burt outside the dressmaker's shop," Nigel said.

"Ay," Avatar agreed. "In my observation of their argument, Ike appeared agitated and offended, while Burt aggressive. Ike may well be a dupe, a name Burt used to cover his actions."

"What about Moreland?" Chad asked, his voice strained in an attempt to keep his anger in check.

"I don't know yet, which is why I wanted to speak with you both. I believe it is time for the King's Champion to pay the farmer an *official* visit to determine what he does or doesn't know about these questionable adoptions."

"Along with the provincial lord and Council Member," Chad added.

"We need an excuse to tell our wives without causing undue stress," cautioned Nigel.

"We always hunt when you visit," Chad brusquely said. "I'll inform Dunsmore to prepare for a pre-dawn departure." He abruptly left.

"Will you tell Mirit the truth?" inquired Avatar.

Thoughtful, Nigel stared after Chad. "No, Chad's reaction is enough to deal with. She'd be a mother badger if she believes anything threatens the children, ours or the orphans." He cast a fretful glance up at Avatar. "The trick will be leaving without her noticing. If she sees me in uniform, she will realize there is no hunt."

"I'll make sure she sleeps extra deep tonight."

Nigel heavily sighed. "I don't like keeping her ignorant but lying isn't an option either when all I want is to keep her and children safe from upset."

Avatar clapped Nigel's shoulder. "I will tell Virgil and Skylar. They know about our investigation."

Chapter 13

THE SUN COMPLETELY CLEARED THE MORNING HORIZON. Moreland made his way to the barn. A short wiry man of middle years with an oblong face, he ran his farm with barking orders to his fieldhands and family. A chorus of *mooos* greeted his arrival. A twelve-year-old boy milked a cow. A full bucket sat beside him. The one beneath the udders appeared at capacity.

"Tomas! You're not done yet?" chided Moreland.

"Sir, I started with Nima, then Tedra, now Bev. The first barrel is already full. They are heavy with milk this morning."

"That is what happens when you miss the evening milking!" Moreland complained.

"Ay, sir." Tomas rose to carry the two buckets to the milk barrels.

"No, take them to the house! It's churning day. Don't you remember anything?"

Tomas sulked at the scolding yet made no reply. The boy had just left when someone grabbed Moreland from behind. The farmer fought back only to come face-to-face with—

"Vance!" Moreland exclaimed with anxiety.

A quick hand covered Moreland's mouth. "Be quiet, you fool!"

Both men's eyes darted to the door, wary of being heard. Nothing. Satisfied Vance released Moreland, though his snarling expression remained.

"You've been slow to act. My father isn't pleased. And neither am I."

Moreland kept his strained voice low. "I told Darnel I would not go to Hagley until the fall harvest is complete. He agreed."

"Plans have changed since their arrival."

"I wasn't told," Moreland complained.

Vance stepped dangerously close. "You *were* told about the children. That should have prompted an earlier visit to Hagley."

Moreland had difficulty disputing the statement, yet still offered up a defense. "I can't just show up at the orphanage with a request for more children. Last time Platt questioned me regarding the number. Fortunately, Burt was there and helped to quiet any concerns."

"We *want* those two. My father didn't appreciate being made a fool of by the girl."

"After morning chores, I'll return to Hagley with my wife. Her added plea might persuade Platt."

"Meet us at the normal place this evening." Vance seized Moreland by the collar. "*And* pray you have good news."

"Master Moreland! Moreland!!" a voice loudly called.

"Stall whoever it is so I can leave." Vance shoved Moreland toward the front barn door. He carefully peeked through slats to see the arriving group.

Moreland barely exited the barn to find an older farmhand pointing out three riders and a Guardian. "Go. I'll take care of this." He shoved the man away to greet the group. "Sir Chad. This is a surprise," he said with a forced smile. "What brings you here, my lord?"

Rather than directly answer the question, Chad said, "Moreland, you remember The King's Champion, Prince Nigel."

Moreland made a hasty bow to Nigel. "Oh, ay. We briefly met last year at the apple festival." He began to look back at the barn but stopped. His nervousness, and halted actions, did not go unnoticed. He flashed an uneasy smile. "It's an honor for The Champion to visit my humble farm. What can I help you with, Highness?"

Stern features matched Nigel's voice in reply. "I will come directly to the point. There are rumors of unsavory characters in the province snatching orphans unaware. *Your* name came up during the investigation."

To this stunning news, Moreland turned to the barn, which prompted Avatar to speak.

"Who is in there?"

"Another farmhand. A young lad. I don't want him to be unduly concerned. He is an orphan," Moreland stammered the hasty response.

Not satisfied by the answer, Avatar moved toward the barn.

"Wait, please! He is a shy, timid lad!"

Avatar ignored Moreland until the farmer dashed in front of him. At that same moment, Tomas returned from delivering milk to the house.

"You, boy! Who are you?" Dunsmore spoke.

Surprised, and uncertain, he spoke in timid voice, "Tomas, sir."

"His son?" Dunsmore motioned to Moreland.

"Eh, no." Tomas shyly lifted the empty buckets. "I help milk the cows."

"Is this the shy lad?" Nigel demanded of Moreland.

The farmer moved to Tomas. "He must have gone out the back without being seen." He quickly said to Tomas, "Run along back to the house."

"Wait," Avatar said. He cast a narrow, inspecting glance to Moreland. Intimidated, the farmer looked away. Avatar softened his approach to Tomas. "Does anyone else help with the milking?"

Tomas swallowed back fear at the Guardian. "No, sir."

At the answer, Avatar entered the barn. Moreland nudged Tomas away before he ran after Avatar. He watched the Guardian make quick search of the stalls. Finding no one, Avatar motioned Moreland to accompany him. Upon return to the group, Avatar shook his head.

Nigel scowled at the silent negative report, and questioned Moreland. "Why did you adopt eight children?"

Moreland spread his arms. "It's difficult to run such a large farm without help."

"You have two sons," Dunsmore interjected.

"Both married. They farm their portion of the land I gave them as wedding gifts."

"Why is Tomas alone with the milking if you have eight others?" Chad asked.

"He's the youngest, and not a strong field worker."

Nigel leaned forward on the saddlebow. Eyes of suspicion direct on Moreland. "Your name is associated with illegal activity. I want to know why?"

Moreland visibly trembled. "I don't know, Champion."

"That's a lie," Avatar declared.

Fear became desperation. When Moreland moved towards Nigel, Avatar intercepted the farmer.

"Please, Champion, I can't speak. Not in the open."

"To the house!" Nigel turned his horse.

To the blustery entrance, Moreland's wife grew fearful.

"Go upstairs, woman!" Moreland ordered.

"No! We will question everyone," Nigel disputed.

"She is not involved. I swear, Highness!" pleaded Moreland.

Nigel's gaze shifted to Avatar. He received an affirming nod from the Guardian. Nigel waved at the wife, "Go."

Once they heard the upstairs door close, Chad asked, "What about your sons? Are they involved?"

Moreland shook his head. "No. It's me alone," he shamefully muttered.

"No," refuted Avatar. "Someone else *was* in barn, but your intervention provided the means to leave. That's why you feared being overheard. He may still be nearby." His jerk on Moreland's arm solicited a nod from the nervous famer.

"You lied about your sons?" Chad demanded.

"No! I tried to keep my family ignorant."

"Darnel?" Chad continued his harsh questioning.

The name caused Moreland great apprehension, yet he curtly shook his head.

"A person associated with him?" Dunsmore pressed.

"Burt?" Avatar asked.

Another careful negative gesture.

Not pleased by the none-verbal answers, Nigel accosted Moreland. "Know this, the King's justice will be swift for those involved. Since you are implicated, cooperation is only way to mitigate the consequences from adversely effecting your family. Do you understand?"

"Ay, Champion," Moreland said in a shaken whisper.

"Now, who was in the barn?"

Moreland forced himself to speak. "Van … Vance."

"Darnel's son," Dunsmore sneered.

"What did he want?" Nigel demanded.

"More … more children. They snatch them to sell," Moreland shamefully admitted.

Chad seized Moreland, his temper on verge of exploding. "You help enslave innocent children! Does he pay enough to silence your conscience?" His grip on Moreland began to choke the farmer.

"Chad!" Nigel warned with concern for his friend.

"*Furasda*," Avatar spoke the Ancient to soothe Chad. He drew Chad back from Moreland.

When Chad appeared to regain his composure, Nigel continued the questioning.

"How are these fake adoptions facilitated? Is Platt involved?"

Moreland couldn't look at anyone. "No. It's done through Burt."

"What about Ike?" Chad asked, his voice strained.

Moreland shrugged. "I don't know about him. All I know, is that whenever Darnel is in the province, he contacts me to place an adoption request."

"Does he give specifics?" asked Nigel.

"Sometimes, but generally he wants those newly brought to the orphanage. Ones that haven't been established yet."

"Did he make a request this time?" asked Avatar.

"Ay. He wanted two. A brother and sister."

"What?" Nigel exclaimed. "Any names given?"

"No. Only they were new and headed this way. Vance did say there was something personal."

Nigel had difficulty calming down. "Dunsmore, take him to the dungeon! Then get troops to arrest Darnel!" To Chad and Avatar, "Back to the manor."

"It may not be them," Chad tried to reassure Nigel.

"But it could be!"

"Virgil and Skylar are with them," Avatar added his encouragement.

Nigel gathered the reins, leapt in the saddle and kicked his horse into a gallop. Chad quickly followed. Avatar placed Moreland on the horse behind Dunsmore before he and the Captain proceeded.

Vance pushed his horse to continue the hard ride. Forty minutes later, he arrived at an old run-down house in Ridley. The family camped behind the house. He abruptly drew rein. The animal bucked, winded and angry. He jumped from the saddle and shouted; "We are betrayed!"

"What do you mean?" demanded Darnel.

"Sir Chad and *The Champion* arrived to confront Moreland. I'm not certain of all that was said, as I left before being discovered."

"Were you followed?"

"No, I'm certain of it. No troops accompanied them, but just the sight of the King's Champion shows someone talked!"

"It wasn't Burt," Colby said.

"How can you be sure?" Vance challenged.

"Because while you went to Moreland, I made the arrangements with him at the orphanage. If they knew about him, he wouldn't have been there."

"So, they *are* at the orphanage," Vance sneered.

"No, still at the manor. Burt will make sure they are here sometime this morning," Colby proudly announced.

"We can't wait. We must leave!" Sophia insisted.

"Not until I have them!" Darnel declared.

"You heard Vance! The King's Champion is aware of us. Is revenge worth our lives?" she challenged him.

Darnel snarled. "Pack up the wagon. You and Genna head northeast to the border. We'll catch up with you."

"But—"

"Do as I say, woman!" He raised a hand as if to strike.

To this gesture, Sophia yielded. However, her summons of Genna became interrupted when the cloaked Guardian suddenly appeared.

"Time is running out," declared the Guardian.

"I know!" chided Darnel. "We are betrayed!" He raised a stiff hand to stop objection. "We're going to get them. The trap has been set, so leave us alone!"

"You forget *who* is giving the orders," the Guardian scoffed.

Undeterred, Darnel rebuffed. "This time it's personal, and I'll do it my way!" He marched toward the house.

"It may not be wise to upset the Guardian," warned Colby.

Darnel went to speak again, only found the Guardian had disappeared.

On a knoll overlooking Hagley, Mona watched. From that vantage point she could see the entire city, and a large part of the surrounding countryside. She observed Nigel and the others leave the city shortly before dawn. As instructed by Avatar, she dispatched Dale. Kendra kept covert surveillance within Hagley.

Mona barely flinched when the cloaked Guardian appeared. Throwing back the hood revealed Dale, who spoke in her regular voice.

"Darnel set the plan in motion."

Mona simply nodded, more focused on the road.

Dale followed Mona's marked attention. She heavily sighed. "For the sake of the children, I look forward to this charade being over."

"All for the cause of justice."

"Ay." Dale cocked a smile to add, "Still, it felt good to rile a few warrior egos in the process."

Mona sent an askew glance to Dale. "Just make sure the goading act ends when the situation is resolved."

Dale simply smiled. "Any word from Kendra?"

"Not yet. Since you provoked Darnel, she should see action soon."

"Will you reinforce her while I return to Ridley?"

"Ay. We best make our moves before too many are awake for the day. Jor'el be with you."

"And with you." Dale replaced the hood. Using the shielding metal, she disappeared.

Chapter 14

Mirit stirred at hearing what sounded like knocking. At first, the voice calling sounded distant. Perhaps, a dream? She sleepily stretched.

"Aunt Mirit?"

Her eyes snapped opened when she recognized Eli's voice. Morning light filled the room. Had she overslept? She sat up to discover Nigel wasn't in bed. She responded to another knock. "Just a moment!"

Once out of bed, she donned a dressing gown to open the door. "Eli. Wyatt," she greeted them with a stifled yawn.

"Morning, Marmi," Wyatt struggled to speak.

She leaned to kiss Wyatt on the head.

"Is Uncle with you? He wasn't in the armory when we went for morning practice."

"Eh, I don't know. Let me check the privy." She admitted Eli and Wyatt before she went to the other room. Empty. "Not here either. It is rather late in the morning, maybe he's at breakfast."

"You don't sound too sure," said Eli.

"It's not like him to let me oversleep."

"We've had so much excitement lately, maybe he thought you could use it." Eli flushed with embarrassment when she looked at him with mild rebuke. "I mean … not that you need extra sleep. No, you look wonderful in the morning. Maybe he did it out of consideration."

Mirit huffed an ironic laugh. "Men. You try to say the right things, yet trip over your own words."

"Marmi pretty," insisted Wyatt.

111

"You learn fast." Mirit ruffed Wyatt's hair. "Now, I'll get dressed and meet you downstairs for breakfast. We'll take a day off from practice."

"She's usually not this agreeable when she oversleeps," Eli commented to Wyatt, as they turned to leave.

"I heard that!" Mirit called from the privy.

In the private morning room, the children assembled for breakfast under the watchful eye of Magan. Servants made certain each child had food. Virgil and Skylar stood in their usual places.

"Good morning, my dear." Mirit greeted Alyson with a kiss on the forehead. "Magan. Boys." She winked at Chandler and Ephrim. Mirit nodded thanks to the servant who set a plate of food before her. She then spoke to Magan. "Why do I assume Chad is somewhere with Nigel?"

Magan sweetly smiled. "He told me before bed that a stag was sighted just north of the city."

"Ah!" said Mirit with understanding. "A hunt," she said to Eli.

He frowned. "It would have been fun to be included."

"Maybe Nigel thought you had too much excitement and needed to sleep," Mirit teased.

Alyson began to laugh but stifled it when Eli scowled.

"Me hunt too," Wyatt said. "Someday," he sheepishly added when Eli looked sideways at him.

"I'm sure you will," said Mirit.

"Since the men are occupied, perhaps an outing," suggested Magan.

"Splendid idea. I haven't been riding yet," said Mirit. Seeing Wyatt and Alyson exchange glances, she asked, "Do either of you know how to ride a horse?"

Wyatt shyly returned to eating, so Alyson replied tentatively. "A little."

When Wyatt wouldn't meet her gaze, Mirit gently added, "Riding is necessary for hunting."

Wyatt glanced curiously to Eli, who affirmed the statement. Wyatt then nodded at Mirit.

Alyson stared with anxiety at her brother. Mirit's touch upon her arm made her turn. "If I have to go," she muttered.

"You don't *have to*. No one will force you, but we usually travel on horseback."

"I know the perfect mounts for you and Wyatt," said Magan to Alyson.

The girl shrugged an *okay*.

"After breakfast then," said Mirit.

Magan rang for Ambrose. She instructed the steward to have the grooms prepare horses and ponies.

Wearing riding attire, Magan and Mirit ushered Alyson and Wyatt to the paddock. The twins wore appropriate clothes for the outing. Eli dressed, as if going hunting, including a sword. Mirit brought her sword, only in a sheath attached to the left front of the saddle. On the belt of her riding habit, she wore a dagger. Magan only wore a dagger.

Magan's horse stood ready outside the paddock with Mirit and Eli's horses. Two fully saddled ponies waited inside the paddock.

Magan smiled at the twins. "These are very tame and friendly ponies. In fact, this one belongs to Ephrim, and the other to Chandler. Chad is teaching them how to ride."

"But they're only three years old," said Alyson.

"I learned to ride when I was three," said Eli.

"I was four when I got my first pony," added Mirit.

"Papa?" asked Wyatt.

"Around that age too," replied Mirit.

Wyatt squared his shoulders. He took the reins to Ephrim's pony and mounted. He proudly smiled.

Determined not to be outdone, Alyson mounted the other pony. When it moved, she let out a small gasp of fright.

Eli caught the pony's bridle. "I'll lead her around the paddock until you feel confident to go solo."

Magan walked around the paddock to keep an eye on the ponies.

Wyatt kicked his pony to follow Eli and Alyson. Mirit began to walk beside Wyatt. "I ride. No …" He pointed to the bridle.

"No help." Mirit smiled and backed off at his nod.

"Loosen up on the reins," Eli instructed Alyson. "Now, relax. She's a very gentle pony."

"How can you tell?"

"By the way she moves, unhurried and undisturbed by your nervousness."

"Ria is very tolerant of Chandler, and you've seen how rambunctious he can be," said Magan with a wink at Alyson.

"Name?" Wyatt patted the pony's neck.

"Ebony, since she's black," replied Magan.

"Nice pony," Wyatt spoke to Ebony.

"Let's try a trot," said Eli. Before Alyson could respond, he began to jog, which made Ria pick up the pace. At first Alyson balked, then settled down. Eli released the bridle. Ria kept moving with Alyson bouncing along. She handled the pace well.

Wyatt kicked Ebony. The pony responded by changing a lope, the gait between a trot and full gallop.

"Not too fast in the paddock, Wyatt," Mirit advised.

He pulled back the reins to a trot.

After several more times around the paddock at a trot, Alyson giggled with enjoyment.

Seeing the girl's reaction, Mirit smiled. "I think we can take our ride now."

Magan opened the paddock gate. Alyson came out first, followed by Wyatt then Eli on foot.

Once Eli and the women were mounted, the group rode to the front courtyard. There they were met by an anxious Archie.

"Lady Magan! Princess!" Archie called, breathless from running.

"What is it, Archie?" asked Magan.

He pointed back. "I just came from town where I went to buy meat and soup bones. Ike told me to give you a message, Princess. It's Corinna." He paused to catch his breath.

"What about her?" asked Mirit, anxious.

Archie took a deep breath to speak. A tremor of hurt filled his voice. "Ike said Burt told him she's dying. Master Platt took her to Doctor Slater because they thought he had new treatment, but ..." He gazed tearfully at Mirit. "She asked about *the kind princess*. That's why Ike sent me with the message."

"Strange Master Platt didn't send word earlier," said Magan, a bit befuddled.

Archie shrugged ignorance. "I just know what Ike told me, my lady."

Mirit swallowed back her own discomposure. "Of course. Where is Doctor Slater?"

Magan replied. "He lives outside of Hagley near a town called Ridley. Better for serving the country folk as well."

With conflicted concern, Mirit glanced at Alyson and Wyatt. "Our ride will have to wait."

"Why? Who is Corinna?" asked Alyson, trying to mask disappointment.

"A little girl who is seriously ill with no cure."

"Why did she ask for you?"

"We visit the orphanage each time we're in Hagley. Corinna has been there for two years."

Disturbed, Wyatt joined his hands together then pulled them apart. "No family ...?"

Though Mirit solemnly shook her head, it was Magan who answered. "Because of her incurable illness, no one wanted her."

Wyatt slumped in the saddle, distraught.

Mirit moved her horse beside Wyatt. "Part of the royal duty is to offer encouragement, comfort, and compassion to those who ask. Do you understand?"

Wyatt nodded. "Marmi help."

"Ay."

"Go with ..." Wyatt motioned between them.

"You want to come?" asked Mirit, a bit taken aback.

"Learn duty be ... cause," he waved at Alyson "Un ... der ... s-t-t ..." He frowned in frustration at being unable to complete his thought.

"We understand what it's like not to be wanted," she finished for her brother.

Mirit's smile quivered at the sentiment. "I would be proud for you to join me."

"You must hurry!" Archie insisted.

"How long does it take?" Mirit asked Magan

"Less than an hour, even at a normal pace." She nodded toward the twins.

Meanwhile at the orphanage, Burt waited near a small window in a supply room on the top floor nearest the street. Anyone traveling to and from the manor had to pass by the orphanage. Ike was with Burt, only impatient as told by his pacing of the room.

"I hope that boy does what I told him," complained Ike.

"Her illness is well known. Besides, Archie trusts you. He'll convey the message," replied Burt, though his focus never turned from the window.

"If she doesn't bring the children, what then?"

"There!" said Burt.

Ike stooped to peer over Burt's shoulder. Magan, Mirit, Eli, and the twins rode pass the orphanage. The Guardians walked behind them.

"It worked!" Ike said with wonder.

"Of course, it did. Archie was the perfect foil, innocent and believable. Now, we must leave immediately! Once Darnel has them, none of us will be safe."

"They already questioned me, and I managed to convince them I had nothing to do with any of this."

"That changed with the adoption."

Curious at the statement, Ike grabbed Burt to stop his departure. "What adoption?"

Burt roughly attempted to remove Ike's hand. The butcher wouldn't be put off. This time he used both hands to grab Burt.

"I said, what adoption?"

"The prince and princess adopted them."

"What?" Ike exclaimed with astonishment. "And you had me—!" He slammed Burt against the wall. "No payment is worth royal wrath!"

"You were already under royal suspicion, and don't pretend otherwise!" At Ike's angry confusion, Burt added, "Fleeing Allon now at least gives us a chance of survival."

Enraged, Ike tossed Burt aside to race from the orphanage.

Once on his feet, Burt limped downstairs. He began to cross the compound when—

"Burt!" Platt called.

Trying to mask anxiety, Burt turned. "Sir?"

Platt stood in the threshold of his office. "Remember, I'm going to the gristmill later this morning. See the children continue their tasks. You know how they get when I'm gone."

"Ay, sir."

Burt waited until Platt returned inside before he rushed out the rear of the orphanage. At the end of the alley, his wife waited with two horses, saddled and loaded with supplies. They headed to the west gate.

117

Chapter 15

C HAD LED THEM THROUGH THE EASTERN GATE INSTEAD OF GOING to the main gate. With the day's activities well underway, they were forced to travel crowded streets to reach the square. The horses breathed hard from the ride thus a bit antsy in navigating the city. From there, they turned up the winding, busy main thoroughfare.

Annoyed by the slowed progress, Nigel snapped, "Avatar!"

The Guardian moved to the front where he shouted for a clear path. People moved aside, some willing, others grousing.

Outside the orphanage, Platt mounted the single horse-drawn cart. He turned at the shouting. He smiled. "Morning, Highness. Sir Chad."

Nigel reined his horse. Angry, he demanded, "What do you know of Moreland's involvement with Darnel?"

The accusatory question made Platt momentarily speechless. He then spied Moreland with Dunsmore. The farmer shied from him. "Highness?" Platt said, unnerved.

"He doesn't know. It's Burt, you should be asking," Moreland muttered.

"Find Burt and bring him to the manor!" Nigel ordered Platt then snapped the reins to continue.

Upon finally reaching the manor courtyard, Dunsmore called, "Sergeant Riston!"

Immediately, a grizzled veteran arrived. "Captain."

"Take this scum to the dungeon!" he said of Moreland.

Riston pulled Moreland from the horse.

Dismounted, Nigel physically halted Moreland. "You better pray it's not my children Darnel wants."

Chad motioned for Riston to continue.

"Father," Archie innocently greeted, as he crossed the courtyard.

"Not now, we have serious business." Dunsmore issued more orders. "Lieutenant Quinn! Assemble a detail to arrest Darnel and his family."

"It's midmorning, so Mirit and Magan are probably with the boys in the nursery," Chad said to Nigel.

Archie overheard. "They're gone, my lord."

The statement made Nigel abruptly stop at the door. He turned on his heels to accost Archie. "What do you mean *gone*?"

The prince's anger made Archie balk. "They left to see Corinna. She's dying."

"At the orphanage?" asked Chad.

"Platt didn't mention that," Nigel refuted.

"No, Ike said Master Platt took her to Doctor Slater in Ridley," Archie tentatively said.

"Ike?" Nigel echoed with anger.

The boy appeared confused and upset. Dunsmore took hold of Archie's shoulder. "Tell us exactly what happened. Leave no detail out."

Archie swallowed trying to regain his composure. "I went to fetch the meat like I've been doing every morning. Ike told me Corinna is dying and that Master Platt took her to Doctor Slater, because he might have discovered a cure. She asked for the kind princess. Ike told me to deliver the message." Growing concerned, Archie watched the different reactions of anger and annoyance.

"Something is wrong because Platt would have told us that," Chad commented to a seething Nigel. He then asked Archie, "Why didn't Platt send word to Magan directly?"

Archie shrugged his ignorance. "Lady Magan asked the same question, but I don't know, my lord. I only know what Ike told me Burt said."

"Burt?" Nigel's ire rose, which made Archie shrink back.

"Ike said Burt told him after Master Platt left." With a worried look on the verge of tears, Archie glanced to Dunsmore. "Did I do something wrong? I just delivered a message."

"He's telling the truth," Avatar said to Nigel and Chad.

Nigel took a breath to calm his temper. "Did Mirit go alone?"

"No. Lady Magan, the young prince, the twins—"

Nigel leapt into the saddle. The horse protested the rough handling. Chad also mounted. Avatar took the lead again.

"To horse!" Dunsmore ordered his men.

Chapter 16

A FEW TIMES MIRIT SLOWED THE PACE WHEN THE DISTANCE widened between her, Magan, and the children. Eli kept pace with the twins. He spoke words of encouragement and instruction. All in all, Wyatt and Alyson seemed to do fine during the ride from Hagley.

Mirit waited for the children to catch up. "You're both doing very well. Papa will proud when I tell him. Not only riding but wanting to help comfort Corinna." She sent a conferring glance to Eli then spoke again to the children. "Continue with Magan. We'll be right behind you."

She waited for Alyson and Wyatt to reach Magan before speaking to Eli. "Since we're unsure of Corinna's true condition, I want you to be ready to take them outside before the worst happens."

"Of course," he agreed.

They hurried their mounts to catch the others.

As usual when traveling with mortals, Virgil took the point while Skylar kept the rear guard. Virgil paused and gripped his sword. His eyes scanned the horizon.

"How much further?" he hastily asked Magan.

"Just around the bend."

"I sense something. Wait here!" Virgil told Mirit before he raced back toward Skylar.

At the same time, Skylar came rushing from the rear. "That patch of woods." He pointed across the meadow.

"We'll escort them to the doctor's for safety then investigate," said Virgil. "At the gallop," he called to Mirit. He waved them on.

"Quickly," she said to Eli, Wyatt, and Alyson.

Skylar and Eli again kept pace with the ponies, while Virgil caught up to Magan and Mirit. Once around the bend, only the roof could be seen since the house was situated in a small dell.

The sense became so strong that Virgil pulled up suddenly. "Take them to the house! We'll deal with the trouble," he instructed Mirit. "Skylar!" he shouted. He drew his sword on the run toward the earlier indicated woods.

"Go on!" Mirit urged Wyatt and Alyson. She watched the Guardians until they disappeared around the bend. She snapped the reins to join the others.

Nearing the dell, more of the house came into view. No smoke rose from the chimney, and all the front windows were shuttered. Mirit urged her horse to the lead, where she stopped.

"Wait!"

Eli helped the twins to stop the ponies.

"What's wrong?" asked Magan.

"I'm not sure. Virgil and Skylar sensed danger and went to investigate. Are you sure this is Doctor Slater's home?"

"Ay. I came here five months ago with Ephrim when he suffered injury during our return from the Temple."

"Then something must have happened because it all shuttered."

Magan curiously observed what Mirit indicated. "Why would we be told about Corinna?"

Mirit didn't reply, as she surveyed the area. "Take the children back to Hagley." She drew the sword from the saddle sheath. "Eli!"

Magan grabbed Mirit's arm. "What are you going to do?"

"Learn why we were told to come here. Now, take them back." Mirit then called to Wyatt and Alyson. She kept her tone neutral. "Return with Magan. Eli and I will be along later."

"Help Marmi!" Wyatt insisted.

Mirit's impulsive smile at the offer quickly faded. "Another time, my brave boy."

"Protect your sister and Magan, as I will Aunt Mirit." Eli drew his sword and saluted Wyatt.

Wyatt pulled out the dagger from his belt sheath to returned Eli's salute.

122

"Thank you," Mirit whispered to Eli.

"I understand his eagerness to help protect."

"Let's hope what we discover isn't as bad as I fear." Mirit kicked her horse to approach the house. Once down the slope to the dell, she shouted, "Hello, the house!"

Although the windows were shuttered, the door stood partially opened. Dismounted, they carefully mounted the steps to the front porch. The sound of weeping came from inside.

"Corinna?" Mirit asked. No response, just more weeping. "Who's inside?" With soft steps, she crossed to the door.

Eli stopped Mirit from entering. "Let me go first."

Mirit didn't object, so Eli pushed the door all the way open. Sword ready, he entered. With the windows closed and no interior lights or fire, long shadows obscured visibility. The only light came from shafts between the shutter slats. The weeping stopped.

Mirit came to Eli's shoulder. "Do you see—?"

Her question was cut short when they were set upon out of the darkness. The momentum knocked Mirit to her knees. Something impacted the back of her head. She went sprawling to the floor, semi-conscious.

Eli saw Mirit go down. Before he could help her, arms grabbed him from behind. He sent a backward elbow jab at the assailant. In the brief struggle to get free, a hard fist clouted Eli sideways. He hit the wall hard and collapsed to his knees.

"Genna, outside!" a male voice shouted.

"We want the children," said another male.

Running feet were quickly followed by the slamming of the door and heavy thud.

Eli hurried to the door. It wouldn't open. He used his shoulder as added force. No good. It wouldn't budge. He paused at hearing the neigh of horses and hooves. At a moan, he made his way to Mirit. "Aunt Mirit?"

She groaned, as she pushed herself onto all fours.

"How badly are you hurt?"

"Headache, but I'm in one piece."

"I heard them say, they want the children. Two men and woman by the sound of their voices."

"Darnel!" Mirit felt to find her sword then stood. She rocked a bit unsteady on her feet.

"They barred the door, and it sounded like they took the horses."

She sheathed her blade to glance around the room. "Find something to smash open a window!"

During his search, Eli tripped in the darkness and fell into a pile of something. "Feels like firewood."

"Hand me a piece." Mirit moved to the closest window. She used the wood to break the glass. She stepped back to let the shards fall to the floor. She then started hitting the shutter as hard as she could. Breathing heavily, she said, "Let's alternate strikes."

After several moments, a hinge cracked. Mirit had no strength left. Eli tried to catch his breath.

"This is too hard," he chided.

"You're stronger than me. Remember, you have some Guardian blood from your father. Strike as hard as you can," she encouraged him.

In preparation, Eli gripped the wood with both hands. With an added shout of determination, he put all his might into the blow. One board fell off.

"Again!" Mirit eagerly said.

Despite breathing hard from effort, Eli made another swing. The shutter burst open. The sudden invasion of light briefly blinded them.

"Well done!" Mirit cheered. Once able to see, she tossed the wood aside to climb out. Eli came next. From the porch, she noticed the horses were indeed gone. "You were right about the horses." She glanced sideway at him. "I hope you run as fast as Tyrone."

"What if I leave you behind?"

"I don't care. We must reach the children." She jumped off the porch and started running.

With swords drawn, Virgil and Skylar raced into the woods. Whatever they sensed seemed to draw them further from their charges. Yet the closer than came to the source, the stronger the awareness.

Skylar seized Virgil to halt their trek. "Guardian?" he asked, disturbed.

"If it is, we have another turncoat. Kell won't like that."

"There's one way to know for certain." Skylar released Virgil. He held his sword in front of his face, took a breath, and summoned his special power. "Heavenly Sight, reveal with your light the enemy," he spoke in the Ancient.

"*Ahhhh!*" Suddenly an outcry came from nearby.

They followed the sound and came upon a cloaked individual on their knees, grunting in pain with burned hands held out. A smoking shielding medal laying on the ground.

Virgil ripped back the hood to reveal a surprising discovery. "Dale?"

With tears of pain on her cheeks, she looked up, pleading. "What did you do to me?"

Enraged, he ignored her question. "Why were you luring us away?"

She grimaced back pain to answer. "Following orders."

"What are you talking about?"

"Please, my hands. Stop the burning."

When Virgil sneered in opposition, Skylar said, "Help her so we get answers."

"Help a turncoat?" spat Virgil.

"No!" Dale looked directly at Virgil, eyes imploring. "Ask Avatar! He knows."

Stunned by the invoking of Avatar, Virgil stared at Dale.

"Her hands," Skylar gently urged.

Virgil sheathed his sword and knelt. She cried out in pain when he took hold of her. "With soothing cold restore that which is on fire." His icy blue eyes glowed when bluish light radiated from his hands to her hands. Soon Dale began to relax, as the pain subsided. When Virgil released her, the skin was completely healed.

"Thank you," Dale breathed with gratitude.

"Now, explain," Virgil demanded.

"We are under orders to deal with Darnel and stop the slave trafficking of orphans. I've been acting as the go-the-between, feeding Darnel bogus information."

"You used a shielding medal to hide your identity." Skylar indicated the smoldering medallion.

"Ay. Kendra is assigned to watch events in Hagley, while Mona keeps an eye on everything else."

"So, when we've sensed a presence, it's been you?" Virgil said more in a statement than actual question.

She nodded.

"But why lead us away from Mirit and the children?" asked Virgil, his anger starting to return.

"Because the plan is in motion, and we needed you away to spring the trap."

Virgil grabbed Dale to get her attention from her hands. "You're using the children as bait?"

Dale shied as she nodded. "Those were the orders."

Virgil bolted to his feet intent on returning.

Dale hurried to catch him. "Avatar and Mona won't let anything happen to the children."

"What about Eli, Mirit, and Nigel?" He shook her off and started running.

Skylar sent a scathing glare to Dale before raced after Virgil.

Chapter 17

Magan tried to urge Wyatt and Alyson, but the ponies could only manage so much speed. Their slow gait was one reason the animals were selected for Ephrim and Chandler.

Alyson fought against crying during the hasty departure. Occasionally Wyatt looked back. When he spotted horses coming around the bend, he drew rein.

"Marmi!"

Alyson and Magan checked their mounts. Alyson had difficulty turning Ria. Magan reached Wyatt first. Her eyes narrowed to focus on the approaching riders.

"That's not Mirit or Eli! Quickly!" She used her reins to hit the rump of Ebony. The pony neighed in protest. It lurched forward then bucked. Wyatt fell off.

Alyson screamed. When Magan turned, she spied a man holding Alyson, who was now on foot.

"Darnel!" Magan shouted. "Let her go, or The Champion will hunt you down."

The riders arrived, Colby and Vance. Colby seized the reins from Magan. Vance dismounted to grab Wyatt, only Wyatt rolled away. He jumped to his feet and pulled out his dagger. The sight made Vance smile with wicked pleasure.

"That wasn't smart, boy." Vance drew his sword.

Alyson screamed, "Wyatt!" when Vance went after her brother.

Wyatt dodged the attack. Being smaller, he avoided a second advance. With a slash, he cut Vance on the left thigh. Angry beyond reason, Vance launched an attack. The force knocked the dagger from Wyatt and sent him back on his rump.

Alyson's second scream became cut short when Darnel covered her mouth. She bit his hand, which led to a momentary release.

"You won't get away from me again!" Darnel sneered and held her harder.

Alyson's cry of pain became muffled by his hand.

When Vance made for another strike, Wyatt shouted and jumped at Vance to tackle him. The momentum made Vance fall to one knee. He managed to shove Wyatt aside.

"Magan!" Chad's shout made her turn.

Spotting Chad, Nigel, Avatar, and Dunsmore with troops, Vance left Wyatt to stand near Darnel. Colby released Magan and moved his horse to shield his father.

Although some distance remained between him and Darnel, Nigel leapt from his horse before the animal stopped. He drew his sword. "Release my daughter! Or you won't live to see the King's justice!"

"I could snap her neck before you move," Darnel threatened.

Wyatt ran to stand beside Nigel. Again, he held his dagger. He pointed the blade at Darnel. "Him! Owner. Protect Alyson."

Nigel's seething rage found Darnel. "So, you're the one responsible for my son's injuries!" He stepped toward Darnel when Avatar stopped him.

"No. Let me." Avatar then confronted Darnel. "You admit partaking in the slave trade of orphans and abuse."

"As my property, I have a right to do as I will," Darnel smugly replied. His jerk on Alyson made her whimper in fear.

"That's all I needed to hear." Avatar drew his sword. He placed the pommel before his face, and spoke the Ancient, *"Guardians, cruinnich!"*

Blinding light emanated from Avatar's sword to engulf the entire area. The mortals shielded their eyes or lowered their heads. A few shouts and gasps came from the direction of Darnel and his sons. The light faded to reveal Virgil, Skylar, Mona, Dale, Kendra, and another Guardian. Dressed in white with a gold breastplate, he held Darnel by the scruff of the collar. Virgil held Vance, and Skylar had Colby. Mona and Kendra had Sophia and Genna.

"Kell?" Nigel marveled. He blinked his eyes into focus.

"Highness," said Kell in acknowledgement.

"Papa!" Alyson ran to Nigel. He sheathed his sword to embrace her.

"Uncle!" Eli arrived, winded but smiled in relief.

Mirit came a few seconds behind Eli. Out of breath, she hugged the children. Eyes of tearful relief upon Nigel.

"Captain Dunsmore, take charge of them," said Kell concerning Darnel and his family.

"With pleasure!" Dunsmore issued orders to his men.

"I take it your arrival has something to do with Avatar's mission," Nigel said to Kell.

Alyson and Wyatt stared in awe at the mighty Guardian captain with the bright gold eyes. Kell tenderly smiled at the twins, which placed them at ease.

"Indeed," Kell replied to Nigel. "There is much to explain. But first," he again looked at the twins, "food and drink to recover from the day's activity. Meat pies, perhaps?" He winked at Wyatt.

"Him funny like the old Guardian," said Wyatt to Nigel.

Avatar coughed to one side at the comparison, which piqued Kell's already amused interest. "He can't say my name well yet," he explained.

"Av-a-tarrr," Wyatt declared.

"Sounds good to me … old Guardian," quipped Kell.

At the manor, Mirit, Magan, and Virgil made certain Alyson and Wyatt were fed and comfortable. Only then, did they join the others in the private parlor.

"Alyson was so exhausted she fell asleep instantly," Mirit told Nigel.

"Wyatt didn't take long either," added Magan.

"With a little Guardian help they will sleep until tomorrow," Virgil happily said.

"Hopefully, so will their parents after hearing this explanation." Nigel nodded at Kell to proceed.

Avatar spoke first. "You know our investigation uncovered the source for the slave trade of orphans."

Nigel swallowed his drink before replying. "I thought you said Platt wasn't involved?"

"He's not. Burt used Platt's upright and gentle nature as cover for his activities."

Kell picked up the explanation. "We managed to stop all avenues of Darnel's network in the other provinces. The North Plains was the only place left. In short, he was *guided* here."

"My Trio was tasked with maintaining his activities to Hagley and the surrounding area," Mona said.

"His accomplishes were still unknown. Thus, I was dispatched to uncover them, and put an end to it," said Avatar.

"Why not include us?" Virgil motioned to himself and Skylar.

"Orders."

At Virgil's scowl to Avatar's answer, Kell spoke. "We needed everyone to be ignorant, thus able to act normal so as not arouse Darnel's suspicion."

"Tell them about me, please." Dale prompted Kell by indicating Virgil and Skylar. He obliged.

"Dale's contrary reputation was broadcast as a cover for her portion of the assignment, with the objective to stop any interference."

Skylar huffed a chuckle. "It worked. If we couldn't avoid her, Virgil would have throttled her."

Virgil's wry grin turned to a brooding frown. "Where do the children come in since Dale said they were bait for Darnel."

"What?" thundered Nigel, his anger instantly piqued.

Kell put up a hand to still Nigel's objection. "We didn't make them bait," he stressed. "Darnel was already on their trail because they escaped him. We simply orchestrated the situation to bring it to a conclusion."

"By putting their lives in danger?" Mirit challenged.

"No," began Mona with reassurance. "When you left Hagley for Ridley, you were never out my sight. I would not have allowed any harm to come to the children."

"That's little comfort," Mirit chided.

"If we had not been involved, the outcome would have been much different," said Kell, pointedly. "The Almighty laid out the whole scenario for the cause of justice, and," he kindly smiled, "as a reward for faithful service."

"What?" Mirit asked, confused.

Kell's smile widened. "In answer to your prayer for children."

A gasp caught in her throat. "This was meant to happen?"

"Ay. The final trap would not be launched until the adoption was complete."

"One of my most joyous tasks was signing the official papers," said Avatar.

Overwhelmed, Mirit sat. Nigel joined her. He too thunderstruck by the revelation. "I don't think either of us know what to say," he muttered in breathy wonder.

Kell's touch made Nigel look up. "Enjoy your family and pass on what you know."

"We can do that," he willingly agreed.

"Tyrone and Tristine are anxious to meet their new niece and nephew."

"They know?" More astonishment for Nigel.

"My orders came from Kell *and* Tyrone," said Avatar.

Nigel nudged a still stunned Mirit. "Sounds like we should return to Waldron."

"Tomorrow Avatar and I will escort you. Tonight, rest, and rejoice that orphans across Allon are now safe thanks to *your* children," said Kell.